Politicians, Potholes & Pralines

Book 6 in
The New Orleans Go Cup Chronicles

Colleen Mooney

Dedication

To the dogs I've loved for their life spent with me,

I will them remember for the rest of mine.

Books in the
New Orleans Chronicles Series

POLITICIANS, POTHOLES & PRALINES is Book 6 in The New Orleans Go Cup Chronicles series.
Copyright © 2019, Colleen Mooney all Editions eBook and Print Edition.
Print Edition

Paperback
ISBN-13: 978-1-7337387-1-2
ISBN10: 1-7337387-1-1

eBook
ISBN-13: 978-1-7337387-0-5
ISBN-10: 1-7337387-0-3

Edited by Dawn Greenfield Ireland.

Chapter One

LANCEY'S RESTAURANT AND bar is one that many in the neighborhood couldn't afford to frequent. This was not the place to celebrate anything ordinary. Lancey's hosted an influential crowd whose New Orleanian blood ran the shade of blue specific to the privileged class.

The clientele included the political elite of the city. Mirrors on the dining room walls allowed patrons to observe every person at every table discreetly. A former mayor eating with several council members was a regular. Their caricatures appeared on the walls over the mirrors along with the famous and infamous New Orleans had to offer. Some were leaders in the community while others' malfeasance left them waiting for indictments or verdicts.

I've known Judge Frances Whitmer since grade school. He made no secret about wanting his caricature on Lancey's wall. He used or abused anyone he thought could help make it happen. After the local news rag published their Annual Best of New Orleans list with Whit as Best New Orleans Judge of the Year, he was sure his face would soon look down into the room. Hence the reason for today's celebration.

My name is Brandy Alexander, and no, it's not a stage name nor am I an exotic dancer or stripper on Bourbon Street. I work in an unglamorous fraud detection unit at a major telecom firm in downtown New Orleans. My gift, or claim to fame, is I can find discrepancies in patterns—from numbers to just about everything.

The traffic from my office on Poydras to Lancey's uptown took twenty minutes via Tchoupitoulas Street, a direct route along the river with only a few traffic lights. Jiff Heinkel, a criminal attorney is the man I am now dating. He is also a friend of Whit's, and was waiting for me to join him in the bar.

Those considered the inner circle and long-standing friends of Whit who worked to get him elected just two short years ago packed the bar area. At thirty-five, he already had made a name for himself as a brilliant trial lawyer for the prosecution. But he wanted the power and prestige only sitting on the bench would give him. He'd run for judge in New Orleans Parish Criminal Court and won.

Whit sat at the bar holding court with his campaign manager and Jiff. When Jiff saw me, he motioned to the bartender. A drink materialized for me by the time I squeezed my way past those vying for an audience with his honor. As I kissed Jiff hello, I felt a tug on my shoulder-length blonde hair from Whit trying to get my attention.

"Well, if it isn't Miss Brandy Alexander," Whit's said in his normal voice, which could be heard over jackhammers busting up concrete. He was at least a foot taller than almost everyone, except NBA players, which helped his booming voice travel, a fact he was oblivious to. My dad once described Whit's six feet seven height as a long drink of water. "If you're ever gonna give me a kiss on the lips, this is the day to do it," his voice bellowed over the din in the bar. His eyes darted over the crowd taking in those arriving, leaving or just watching, "I'm really popular today."

"Never gonna happen," I said leaning into Jiff. I nodded to Whit's campaign manager, Justine—soon to be wife number four. She had a perpetual stoic expression on her face that never showed a hint of emotion. Could it be Whit's attraction to Justine had to do with her name? It wouldn't surprise me since he named his dog, Justice.

"Get over here, we're saving a seat just for you, baby. That alone deserves a kiss," he boomed over me until I gave him a peck on the cheek in greeting.

Justine was the love interest du jour. She started as his campaign manager and had been elevated to his law clerk. Her job consisted of getting him to meetings on time, home after celebrating, like tonight, or after the endless political dinner parties on his agenda. I imagined her driving skills were not the only thing Whit appreciated about her. She was Chinese, smart and twenty something. Add a facial expression that made it impossible to know what she was thinking, plus she was tall, brunette and wore expensive clothes that showed off her dynamite figure.

Tonight, she wore a body-hugging sheath in a nude color which made her appear, well…nude. While Justine and I are the same height, 5'9", I'm blonde and have what many consider a great figure. Men didn't walk into walls looking over their shoulder at me, like they did staring at Justine's exotic beauty.

Justine decided it was time to go. As she ushered Whit by the elbow to the door, he boomed, "Don't stay out late, all of you. Monday is a school night. There's a long week ahead of us."

He glad-handed all his pals who showed up to celebrate with him on the way out. I spotted August Randolph and Pierre LeBlanc, two of Whit's golfing buddies with serious looks on their faces as Whit shook their hands. They both left moments after Whit and Justine.

There were quite a few friends and colleagues who only showed up to stay in his good graces. Whit had a big mouth and would broadcast anything he thought would make someone uncomfortable under the guise of a joke. Many did not find him amusing.

Jiff and I stayed awhile and finished our drinks. When we started to leave, I noticed Whit's jacket on the back of my chair. I picked it up and checked the pockets to make sure he didn't leave his wallet or keys in one. I found a cellophane-wrapped praline in a side pocket. It was from his run for office and said 'Whitmer for Judge' on the wrapper.

"I'll drop it off to him," I said to Jiff as we made our way out the door. "It's on my way home." Jiff put his arm around my shoulders and even with four-inch heels, he towered over me by three inches.

"Brandy, it'll take you an hour," Jiff said rolling his eyes. "Getting past the security gate and in the front door adds fifteen minutes to your stop. Gracefully avoiding an invitation to have yet another celebratory drink, will require a couple of white lies and a lot more time." He kissed me good night and added, "Try not to get sucked in. I'll call you later."

🐈 🐈 🐈 🐈 🐈 🐈 🐈 🐈 🐈 🐈

I WAITED IN the driveway for the gates to open after I punched in the security code of Whit's home. He's been using the same code since high school—007. I was about to call his cell when I noticed the front door ajar by several inches. Something was off. If nothing else, Whit's dog, Justice should be running around barking in the yard. Then I saw the security system had not automatically closed and locked the iron gate.

When I got to the massive leaded glass front door, I pushed it open with the back of my hand far enough to step inside. The security panel appeared to be disarmed. Typically, it would blink displaying the green light if armed.

I had the feeling of being watched which made me look up to the top of the stairs. Claudette, the judge's second and third ex-wife—Whit married her, divorced her, remarried her, then re-divorced her was standing with her hands on her hips staring down at me.

"Claudette, what are you doing here? You scared me half to death," I said while my hand flew to my chest. The staircase in the grand center hallway started at the end of the first two rooms. The landing set it back two more rooms overlooking the beveled glass front doors and marble foyer.

"I could ask you da same thing," she said in her unmistakable y'at accent indicative of native New Orleanians.

"I stopped by to drop off Whit's jacket. He left it at the restaurant," I said and held up my arm with the jacket draped over it by way of proof. "When I got here both the gate and front door were open and the security system isn't on." I said. "Did you disarm it?"

"The alarm was already off. I came in da kitchen and went up da back stairs," Claudette said. "He was probably drunk when he got home and forgot to lock up when he left to take Justice for a walk."

"Whit's not here?" I asked and noticed the doors to his study just off the foyer were closed. That's odd, I thought. I've never seen that door closed in all the years I've been coming to this house.

"His office door is closed," I said. "Don't you think that's odd?"

"Whit is odd.," she said. "I'm here for my son's tuition money he's supposed to have sent me a week ago. Whit is always late sending it. I want to get it and leave before he gets back." Claudette had a fiery temper and once she revved it up, it was hard to throttle down.

"Was Justice here?" I asked. "Did you see or hear him when you came in the back?" I asked wondering if Justice ran out the front door and gate.

"Some watchdog. You'd think he'd at least bark at me. Dat dog never liked me," she said turning to go to one of the upstairs rooms.

"Wait," I said a little too loudly, but it made Claudette stop.

"Whit is probably stumbling around da neighborhood taking his precious Justice for a stroll," she snarled.

"So, you haven't seen Whit or Justice?" I asked. A cold feeling crawled up my back. Whit never left the alarm off when he wasn't home. All of us knew the code and just let ourselves in if he was expecting us. He only turned it off if he was home and let someone in.

"How many times I gotta tell you dat?" she snapped and puffed out a breath.

Claudette stood at the top of the stairs while I opened the massive office doors that were normally left pocketed into the wall on either side.

"Whit!" I gasped when I saw him face down on the floor in a pool of blood. His hands were tied behind his back. I didn't need to touch him to know he was dead.

Chapter Two

EVERYTHING MOVED IN slow motion after I discovered Whit on the floor. Whatever Claudette was saying from the top of the stairs sounded like the warning barks of rhesus monkeys jabbering to their tribe of an incoming predator. In front of me were bloody paw prints all around Whit. He was face down in front of his desk on the hardwood floor with blood pooling around his body.

I closed the doors to the crime scene and concentrated on my breathing for a moment. A flash that Claudette might be the killer brought me abruptly back to listening to her when she spoke.

When I looked up at the top of the stairs, I caught a glimpse of her going down a hallway.

"Claudette, wait," I said. I started up the stairs after her.

"I let myself in here to get what he owes me—our son's school tuition. You gotta problem wit dat?" Claudette hissed at me when I caught up to her. She was a good-looking woman who tried too hard. She was a brunet, same as Justine, with long dark hair she had permed within an inch of its life. She had a great figure which she showed off with tight, ankle length, black Lycra pants, four-inch black stilettos and a V-neck, super tight Lycra blouse. It ensured the viewer wouldn't miss her cleavage from fifty feet away—in a fog. Up close they looked like they were auditioning for The Great Escape. Her hair was too big and her clothes too tight.

I didn't think she could see into Whit's office or see Whit on the floor when I opened the door. Claudette was ultra-self-absorbed so she didn't notice my reaction to seeing him.

I wasn't sure how Claudette would take finding out Whit was dead, and I didn't want to be the one to tell her. My gut told me she had no idea he was dead in his study, and that she had nothing to do with it. She would have been screaming hysterically if she knew or even fallen down the stairs in a faint had she seen him. I needed to get her downstairs and wait in the parlor with me while I called 911.

Claudette turned on her heel to face me when I put my hand on her shoulder as I caught up to her. She raised her shoulders and let out a huff. "My lazy ex-husband can remember every sentence rendered on every scumbag in this city, but he can't remember to mail his son's tuition to the school on time."

My throat was dry when I tried to talk. I cleared it and asked her, "How did you get in? It didn't look like you came in the front, did you?" I stood rubbing my hands together like you do when there's only the air dryer and no paper towels in the ladies' room.

"I already told you I came in da kitchen, and up da back stairs to da master bedroom. Why? What's wrong with you?" she eyed me wringing my hands.

"Then where did you go?" I asked.

"Dat is none of your business, but I was about to leave when I saw you walk in from up here."

"Why the master?" I asked.

"I wanted to see if he had any cash in his safe," she said with an exaggerated eye roll. "He keeps a stash there, usually a lot if he's been winning."

"Show me," I said. If I wanted any information on what Claudette was doing or where Justice might be hiding, I needed to get it now before I called the police.

"I don't have to," she said, folding one arm across her chest, and she reached for and started twisting a strand of her long, wavy, dark brown hair.

I'd seen her curl her hair around her finger since high school when the nuns called on her and she was unprepared with the correct answer.

"Where's the safe?" I asked.

Claudette answered in a defiant stance with an exasperated huff.

I put my hands on my hips and said, "It's important."

She raised her chin, stuck it out and strode off down the hall.

I followed.

At the door of the master bedroom an oil painting of Whit was on the floor slashed to pieces. Directly above it was an open steel door that showed the empty safe set in the wall. The faded paint around the safe looked to be the same size as the slashed portrait. I assumed Whit's likeness had hidden it.

There were photos of Trey, Whit's son in his khaki Jesuit uniform with the Blue Jay patch on the sleeve. Trey is what the French here use for the third. Claudette's family is French and while her son was Frances Whitmer III, he went by Trey. Their younger son is ten years old and in private Catholic Grade School when he's not in rehab. I imagined his picture in a prison jumpsuit rather than a Jesuit uniform being added one day next to Whit, his dad and Trey in their Jesuit uniforms. Now, it didn't look like the photos over the fireplace mantle in Whit's master suite would acquire any additions.

"Miss Nosy, before you ask, I didn't open it. It was like dat when I got here," she said. "And empty."

"You have the combination?" I asked looking around the room.

"Of course. Anyone who knows Whit, knows his combinations and passwords. Combinations are 007 and his passwords are always his best golf score, a 73 with the date he played it…on his birthday, November eleventh," she smirked. "The safe combo is 11-11-73."

"And that oil painting? Was it like that?" I nodded to the oversized likeness of Whit or what was left of it.

"No, dat's courtesy of me. I giveth and I taketh away," she said putting her hands on her hips and pushing her head back so her chin pointed at the ceiling.

"What did you slash that with?" I asked looking around for a weapon.

"Well, Nosy Nellie, if you must know, Whit keeps scissors in da night stand. He uses it to cut photos out of his porn magazines or print-outs he puts in his wallet until he finds a new one he likes better. He is a creature of habit, and the scissors were still there," she said with her arms crossed and tapping a foot. "Before you ask…I put 'em back."

Porn. Too much information—something I didn't need or want to know about Whit. However, this type of info usually raised its ugly head again when it was least opportune.

"Where's the money you thought he had for your son?" I asked. "Or do you think someone came in here and robbed him?"

"It probably paid off a gambling debt," Claudette said as her shoulders slumped and she deflated sinking down onto the bed. "You remember how he was in high school? He'd bet on everything, like whether da lunch room would run out of macaroni and cheese, and it only got worse in college. Now, it's only golf games he bets on with friends. Some friends though. They all know he has a problem and they take advantage of him."

"I do remember. Once in high school we came here to pick you two up on the way to a dance or a movie. His dad was screaming at him over losing a bet," I said. "I thought he outgrew it or learned from that lesson."

"His dad paid dat debt off and many others. I remember you being here for dat one. Whit lost over $5,000.00 at the Racetrack he borrowed from one of his rich friends. His dad had to pay it back," she said. "He never got better, only worse, losing more and more each time." Claudette exhaled in defeat.

"So, how does he afford to stay in this house? I guess the better question is how has he not had to sell it to pay off a debt?" I asked while my mind replayed the vision of Whit downstairs in a pool of blood. If I didn't get info out of Claudette now before she saw Whit, I wouldn't get anything useful after she saw his dead body.

"The only reason Whit has not gambled away dis house is because his parents left all their money in a trust for Whit or his children to inherit. Whit could live here until he dies, then the house goes into a trust for his children or grandchildren. The cash or other assets will go to our two boys when they reach twenty-one or earn a college degree. They even took care of him after they died so he didn't wind up homeless," she said.

"Whoa, I had no idea," I said.

"There's nothing for me here, and I want to be gone when he gets home. If he's out walking Justice, he'll be home soon," she said and stood up to leave.

"Come with me downstairs, I need to show you something," I said and turned to head back down the stairs.

"Do you want him to catch me here?"

I didn't think Claudette could have killed him and then parade me around the house talking about Whit's interest in porn, gambling debts and the tuition he owed her. "Whit is home," I finally eked out. "We need to call the police, and you need to come downstairs with me and wait for them."

"Why do I need to wait for them? I didn't take anything. Is he putting you up to getting me to tell you why I'm here?" Claudette stormed down the staircase ready to take on Whit as she pushed open the sliding pocket doors. I tried to stop her before she thundered into his office. She stopped when she saw him on the floor. I grabbed both her arms to keep her out of the crime scene.

"Let go of me...I swear..." she said. But the longer she looked at Whit in the bloody mess, her knees buckled as she crumbled into a sobbing heap on the floor. "Oh no...no...no," was all she managed between sobs.

"C'mon, Claudette. Let's sit in the parlor while I call for the police," I said helping her to her feet.

"Police? I'm not waiting for da police. I'm getting outta here," she turned toward the back door but the shock of seeing him had her rooted in place.

"You know I have to call the police and tell them you were here," I said. "It would be better if you stayed and tell them yourself."

"You're right, but they're going to think I did it," she said between the blubbering. "I loved Whit. Even with all the things we said and did to each other, I would have taken him back, again. I couldn't kill him even though I probably said it a dozen times."

I seemed to remember she said it more like a million times.

"I know," I said. I put my arm around her shoulder easing her back to the parlor and over to a chair to wait while I called 911 from my cell.

Chapter Three

AFTER I PLACED the 911 call, I called Jiff Heinkel. Jiff and I had been dating since we met, in typical New Orleans fashion, at a Mardi Gras parade. The details of that meeting are a lot more complicated and involve a steamy lip lock we exchanged even before I knew his name.

Jiff was an attorney with his dad's criminal defense firm. He knew Whit from high school. They attended Jesuit together. He knew Claudette, too, over the many on again, off again splits in their relationship and the reconciliations during both their marriages. I thought Claudette might benefit from getting Jiff to represent her.

"Jiff," I said lowering my voice so Claudette couldn't hear what I said. "Can you meet me at Whit's house right now? His security gates and doors were open." I walked away from Claudette but stayed between her and an exit before I added, "I found him in his office, on the floor in a lot of blood. I think someone murdered him."

"He's dead? Was he shot?" Jiff asked.

"I'm not sure. I can only see a pool of blood he's lying in so I'm not sure and I don't want to touch anything," I said.

"No, don't touch anything. I'm on my way," he said and hung up.

I made a quick call to my roommate, Suzanne asking her to let Meaux out one more time before she left for work. Suzanne worked nights as an exotic dancer making a lot more money in tips than I did at my day job. She went to the University of New Orleans School of Engineering during the day and had one semester left before graduating. She grew up with five brothers and said taking her clothes off in front of men was no big deal—her words, not mine.

"Hey, Brandy," she answered on the first ring. "I'm walking out the door. What's up?"

"Can you let Meaux out for me before you leave? I'm going to be late. I stopped at Whit's to drop off a jacket he left at Lancey's and I found him dead on his office floor," I said. Suzanne had dated Whit all of a second in high school until Claudette gave her the evil eye. Suzanne's mantra was "No man is worth fighting another woman over."

"Oh, no," she said and paused. "Heart attack or did he vex the wrong woman and find himself on the losing end of an argument?"

"Looks like the latter, and now I'm waiting for the police."

"Whit wasn't the kind who would have had a heart

attack. He would have given a heart attack to someone else," she said. "What about his little dog?"

"He's missing. I hope he turns up okay somewhere," I said and put the worst-case scenario out of my mind.

"Well, if anyone can find him and help the police with who killed Whit, it would be you…even if they don't realize they need your help," she said adding, "Be careful. Whit made a lot of enemies sitting on the bench, and a whole lot more from his evening shift, a.k.a. dating life. I'll feed Meaux too in case you're really late."

"You are the best," I said, and we hung up.

As I finished the phone call, I noticed the answering machine blinking on Whit's desk in his office.

"Claudette, do you know how to access Whit's answer machine remotely?" I asked.

"Maybe. Yeah. Probably. I'm not sure," she said between sniffles and blowing her nose into a tissue. "I doubt he changed it."

Claudette was still crying, and I tried to get her to focus on something else.

"Whit never changed his codes on anything. I'm sure it's still 007, or if he needed a four-digit code, he just added another zero to it. That's how I let myself in. Why?" she asked.

"Well, I see it blinking on the desk in his office and am wondering who was trying to reach him," I said.

"It's probably Mavis Martin or his new hottie, his

law clerk, Justine. Mavis and Bas are divorced. Whit has been hot for her since we all were at LSU," Claudette said flipping off sadness and flipping on anger. Then, she cried some more.

"Mavis and Bas are separated?" I asked. Bas was Judge Sebastian Martin, but we all called him Bas. He sat on the bench in criminal court, same as Whit. Whit and Bas had been friends since they both attended Jesuit, an all boy, Catholic high school.

"No. Divorced," Claudette said. "Bas caught Whit and Mavis coming out of the hotel elevator at the Fairmont one evening on his way to meet friends in the Sazerac Bar. Talk about bad timing for Mavis. Just about the time the ink was dry on their divorce Whit moved on to Justine."

"Wow, Mavis had to be devastated," I said. "How did you find out all this?"

"Bas called me to tell me he saw them in the Fairmont and that he was filing for divorce," Claudette sniffed and wiped at her eyes. "He wanted me to hear it from him. I was more devastated finding out about Mavis with Whit. She knew I wanted to reconcile with him. I thought she was my friend."

"What ever happened to Whit's first wife?"

"They were married all of five minutes. It was more of a hot date than a marriage. The divorce took longer to finalize than the time they were married," she said.

"It takes longer to plan a wedding then get out of one," I said.

"Yeah. She was also a friend of Mavis' at LSU. When Whit couldn't have Mavis, he went for Jennifer something. I don't remember her last name. She and Mavis were Golden Girls for LSU. They looked a lot alike."

"I didn't go to LSU and didn't know Mavis and Bas in college. What did she and Jennifer look like?" I asked.

"The LSU Golden Girl look. Tall, lanky, and model thin with big boobs. They both had long dark hair and dark eyes. If you've met Marigny, Bas and Mavis' daughter, she's an exact duplicate of Mavis when she was at LSU."

Wow, I thought Claudette didn't realize she could have been describing herself. She looked a lot like Mavis and Jennifer what's her name. Whit definitely had a type.

"What happened to Jennifer, the first wife?" I asked.

"She bugged out of Baton Rouge and moved back to where she was from, Connecticut, I think, when she realized Whit's gambling problem," Claudette said.

"Then you two married?"

"Yeah, and divorced, then married again. I should have had shock treatments after the first divorce so I'd never contemplate doing it again. I loved him. I had a child with him so I thought I'd give it another go. He agreed to let me handle the money. He never stopped gambling, which meant I had to pay those debts along with the bills," she said. "Instead, we had a second child together, and I hoped that would change him."

Why do women assume adding children to a stressed-out relationship will improve it especially with a big kid like Whit, who had no sense of responsibility?

Before I could grill Claudette further about the Mavis and Bas divorce—a shocker to be sure—a crack of thunder sounded like it was in the living room, followed by a fierce downpour. That's a typical rainstorm for spring in New Orleans. It came down in buckets and Claudette and I looked out the windows to see if the streets were flooding. I had parked in the driveway so I wasn't worried for my car, but when uptown streets flood, the water could come up over the wheels of cars left parked on the streets.

While we watched the rain water building in the street, a blinding sea of blue flashing lights arrived and flooded every uncovered window pane and beveled glass across the front of the house. Since I had left the front door like I found it, the first person I came face to face with was Captain Dante Deedler rushing inside to get out of the rain. A little too close behind him was his old partner Detective Hanky. Her new partner, Detective Travis Taylor followed her at a safe distance and was wearing rain gear.

Dante stopped in his tracks when he saw me causing Hanky to run smack into his back shoving him into me so that our chests smashed together. He grabbed me by both arms. Hanky had been looking over her shoulder at Detective Taylor who watched the whole thing unfold. He looked amused, a twitch of a smile threatened the corners of his mouth. I could feel my face getting hot from the blush creeping up my neck.

Detective Travis Taylor was tall, fit, and I found him very attractive and he made no secret he found me "interesting." He transferred to the New Orleans Police Department from Brooklyn, the Bronx, somewhere out of the New York City Police Department. Rumor had it, he had been a detective working undercover in violent crimes and human sex trafficking.

He asked if I would go out with him once. But since he worked for Dante—and my history with Dante is complicated to say the least—I didn't think it would ever be wise for either of us to date or even appear to be dating. Besides, he was a Yankee.

The last time I saw Dante was on Christmas Eve about four months ago. He schemed with Woozie and my dad to get me to his parents' home where he proposed in front of everyone. Two things made that the most awkward moment of my life, not only for me but for everyone there, except Dante.

One—I was on my way to meet Jiff, the man I was dating, and his family to spend Christmas Eve with.

Two—I couldn't believe Woozie and my dad conspired to put me in such a compromising position. Okay, there's at least three things.

Three—This was totally unexpected since I hadn't seen Dante for weeks. Correction…months before Christmas. There had been one or two sporadic phone calls which always ended abruptly because of another dead body or his inability to courteously or politely end a phone conversation.

Right after he popped the question, everyone, and I mean everyone, had looked at me and waited for my answer. Then—I could kiss her for this—Hanky stormed through the front door oblivious to what was going on, and said, "Captain we have a multiple homicide you're needed for. It involves Clayton Haines."

Clayton Haines was a drug lord responsible for several mass shootings, and on Christmas Eve he had orchestrated another one involving multiple bodies for one night.

Dante popped up off one knee, handed the ring to one of his brothers, and bolted out the door after Hanky like someone fired him out of a cannon. He left me standing there in front of everyone waiting for my answer to his big question. While everyone was staring out the front door after him, I turned and walked out after them, got in my car and joined Jiff as planned.

Needless to say, everyone, and I mean everyone, in both families expected me jump for joy at this development, when, in fact, I hadn't seen or heard from Dante since before Thanksgiving. He called once to tell me he was at a Captain's conference in Houston and would not be home for Christmas. He told me via a brief phone call during a conference break I should make other plans for the holidays. He didn't think the conference would end in time for him to get a flight home.

He didn't wait for my answer. He hung up or he would have heard I already had other plans. Everyone in my family and Dante's has been and remained royally ticked off at me, especially my mother. I had noticed Dante's mother was crying happy tears over this long-awaited moment when I got there which turned to wailing when Dante left with Hanky. I followed them out the door.

Clayton Haines was the drug kingpin in New Orleans who was behind bars since New Year's. Even from behind bars, he ordered hits on anyone who even thought of testifying against him.

Whit had instructed the jury they could render a sentence of lethal injection. The jury was out for only one hour on the same day. They returned a guilty verdict on all multiple counts of first-degree murder including multiple rapes, killing of multiple witnesses, and a New Orleans Police Officer. They also agreed unanimously on death by lethal injection. It was a landmark trial, and we all had celebrated hoping that the crime spree gripping the city was being brought back under control.

Hanky brought me back to Whit's living room straightening her jacket while saying, "Captain, I'm sorry. I didn't see you stop. I was looking over my shoulder taking to..." She trailed off when she saw me. She didn't know whether she should apologize to me for causing the collision or not. Dante wasn't sure he should apologize for the body slam so he looked around and told Hanky, "I'll start in there until forensics gets here," indicating where I found Whit.

Detective Travis Taylor stopped without barging into anyone. He stood behind Hanky smiling at me.

"Detective Taylor, I'd like to make a statement on what happened when I got here. Do you want to take it?" I didn't really want to speak with Dante over this with so much left unsaid between us.

"Yes, let's go talk in here," he said and ushered me into the parlor where Claudette was waiting and crying. Hanky followed us and asked Claudette to go with her to the kitchen to make her statement.

"Do you think I should wait for Jiff Heinkel, my attorney, to get here before I say anything to you?" I asked Detective Taylor when we stood in the parlor alone. "And stop smiling."

"It's curious that you turn up at every hi-profile case our Captain is called out on," he said. "You even get here before he does. I find that amusing. Maybe you just want to run into me?"

"Maybe I'm stalking you," I said.

"Funny, I've never noticed you. Perhaps you should stalk me a little closer," he said and took a step closer so he was standing in my personal space. "And please call me Travis instead of Detective Taylor. Most stalkers feel a closeness to their target to at least call them by their first name."

Detective Taylor was a lot better at calling me out than I was at calling him.

"Well, Detective Taylor, all of us know each other from high school, and in some cases, like the judge in there, I've known since grade school. It's not unusual that we all run in overlapping social circles," I said and stepped back.

"How well did you know that judge?" Taylor asked raising his eyebrows while looking me in the eye. This was getting my dander up.

"We weren't connected like that," I said. I crossed my arms across my chest and continued, "Girlfriends of mine dated him and we all sort of hung out at football games, dances, or parties. It's a New Orleans thing. I bet it's harder to bump into people you grew up with in New York, Brooklyn or Pluto, wherever you're from."

"Hard, but not impossible," he said. "So, are you going to tell me why you're really here?"

"Yes, I'll tell you…but it's a boring tale up until the point I found him on the floor." I took a deep breath to calm myself before I continued. "Earlier this evening, we were all at Lancey's. Whit, the judge, the dead one in the other room, had left Lancey's with his fiancé when I noticed his jacket was on the back of my chair. I drive past here on my way home so I figured I'd drop it off to him. Just trying to do a friend a favor," I said.

Jiff would probably give me an earful about talking to the investigating detective without him being present but Detective Taylor, his partner, Hanky and I all had a history together. I had helped them on a case or two in the past and I would hope he'd know better than to suspect me.

I gave Detective Taylor the details. This consisted of how we came to meet at Lancey's, returning Whit's jacket and how I found both the gate and front door open with Claudette standing at the top of the stairs. I told him what we did after I saw Whit in the study, and that I noticed the bloody paw prints around Whit but I haven't found Justice.

"What do you mean you haven't found justice?" he asked scribbling away with his Mont Blanc pen on his leather-bound notebook.

"Justice is the name of the judge's dog and he's nowhere to be found. I'm trying to find him. I'm not seeking moral rectitude for his murder. That's your job. The dog is missing. When I opened that door and found Whit, I noticed the bloody paw prints around Whit's body, but they don't run away from him. I think someone picked Justice up and took him with them."

"Right. You and the dog. It figures," he said.

"Not just any dog. It's a schnauzer and one the judge adopted from me," I said.

Taylor stopped writing, tilted his head back, and rolled his head and eyes at the same time. I struggled not to laugh at him because he looked so funny and out of character.

I did a breed-specific dog rescue for schnauzers.

Taylor was aware of this since his partner, Hanky, adopted Valentine from me and he had to hear how wonderfully smart Valentine was on many occasions.

"Why would someone take the dog with them? Was Justice a friendly dog?" Taylor asked.

"He was friendly enough, let people pet him and pick him up. He never bit anyone that I'm aware of, but he's a schnauzer and a barker," I said. "So, if someone killed Whit and left, the dog would run out barking after him and draw attention from the neighbors."

"Well, would he let someone pick him up and carry him out?" Taylor asked looking puzzled.

"Probably, if he knew the person but I'm not sure he'd let the person who just killed his owner. Justice wouldn't have been too friendly. They could have thrown a coat or towel over him. Then, they could have picked him up."

"Did you see anyone else coming or going when you arrived?" he asked.

I noticed His Gucci-ness had on an expensive Rolex Submariner, Italian loafers—the kind with thin soles—and a light-weight wool, Armani suit. I wondered how does he afford to dress like this on a detective's salary. I knew what Dante made, and he bought his clothes, suits and all, from JC Penney—off the rack.

"The judge left Lancey's with Justine—his fiancé—who gave him a ride home," I said.

"Justine? His fiancé's name is Justine? Now, you're

just messing with me," Travis said and stopped writing.

"No, that's her name, Justine. Justice is the dog. Justine is the girlfriend," I said. "You are very quick, Detective Taylor to pick that up on the first pass."

"How do we get in touch with this Justine?" he asked acting as if he wasn't amused, but I knew he was, given the snappy repartee of our exchange. He had an ever so slight upturn of his lip he fought to control.

"She's his law clerk and works at the courthouse. I was a little surprised she wasn't here when I arrived. We only stayed about an hour longer after they left Lancey's together," I said. "We, as in my boyfriend, Jiff Heinkel, who is on his way here."

"Of course, our Captain's nemesis," Taylor said, then asked. "Do you think the ex-wife, the one talking with Hanky, could've done it?"

"I considered that when I saw the body, but no. She was at the top of the stairs when I got inside. We sort of surprised each other. She said she came in the kitchen door so we didn't see each other. I don't think she has it in her to kill Whit, then walk around with me like she owned the place. Claudette has difficulty maintaining control of her emotions."

Taylor's eyes looked up at me from his notes. His head stayed down and his pen was still on the paper.

"Wait, that didn't come out right. What I meant to say is I don't think she would've been in control when I saw her if she had just killed Whit. I've known Claudette since high school and she isn't that good of an actress. She doesn't act as much as she reacts…to everything."

"You'd be amazed at how fast someone can put on a good show when they think they're going to be arrested for murder," he said.

"She came apart when I opened that door and she saw Whit in all that blood on the floor. I don't think she could have done it and maintained her composure. She told me she was still in love with him."

"Ex-wife still in love with her ex-husband who is about to marry someone else—the hot, sexy, law clerk?"

"I didn't say Justine was hot and sexy."

"You didn't have to. Given the choice, I don't think any man will hire the unattractive one," he said.

"Men are pigs?" I asked. "Are you confessing?"

"Sex, love, betrayal, and money. All the reasons the ex looks good for this," Taylor said and closed his notebook and looked me square in the eye holding his stare a bit too long.

"It's easy to believe she'd want to kill him if you knew Whit. Claudette married him twice," I said trying to make a stronger case for her.

"Oh, God, now she has twice the reasons she'd want him dead," Taylor said smiling.

"Yes, she had double the reasons anyone else could have had to want him dead, but she would have married him again. Your suspect list will be long with just the women he has wronged, not to mention the convicts in prison with a grudge. Let's not forget

Clayton Haines and his band of thugs. Claudette still loved him. She told me she would have taken him back for a third time. You're wrong. She didn't do it. And neither did I, in case you were going to ask."

Chapter Four

J IFF ARRIVED AND after briefing him on the current events I asked him if he would represent Claudette.

"I can't. I got a call on the way here from Bas who asked me to represent him," Jiff said as he pulled me aside.

"What? That seems super-fast for Bas to find out Whit's dead since I just called the police, then you."

"The officer on desk duty contacted him after your call came in. Someone will reach out to all the judges on the bench so they can exercise caution. When something happens to one, they fear it could happen to another. They sent a squad car to Bas' house for safety. He also said he's afraid when the police find out that Mavis was dating Whit, they will want to question him and her. He wants me to represent him," Jiff said. "Did you hear Whit was dating Mavis?"

"Just found out about an hour before you did," I said. "Bas wasn't at Lancey's and I thought that was odd, being old friends and all."

"Not so friendly as of late," Jiff said. "I don't know yet, but since he divorced Mavis, Bas heard rumors that

Whit had been seeing Justine, even before he and Mavis separated. He's really ticked at Whit for ruining his marriage with Mavis only to dump her at the curb for Justine."

"You'd think he'd feel Mavis got what she deserved," I said.

"Some of the courthouse employees have heard the two of them yelling at each other in their chambers over it. Bas wanted to work it out for the sake of their daughter. He hoped they would reconcile, but Mavis doesn't want to," Jiff said.

"Claudette told me she was aware Whit was dating Mavis, and that was the reason for their divorce. I was trying to get her to dial in and remotely get those messages blinking on the answer machine when the cavalry arrived. The police will find out soon enough if Mavis or Bas left one of those messages," I said.

"I'll get a copy of any messages on the answering machine if Bas gets arrested since I represent him. Brandy, don't you think you should take a step back," he said lowering his voice and nodding toward Dante. I didn't look in Dante's direction.

Jiff knew I grew up next door to Dante, and the poorly kept secret that both of our families had always expected us to marry. He heard all of it, right up to the part where Dante had proposed on Christmas Eve. That, I left out. I had not seen that coming. I had told Dante we were done when he got up the nerve and drifted over to my house right before New Years Eve.

He figured I had enough time to cool off after his hasty departure on what everyone in both families thought should be the most important moment in my, not our life. I had not told Jiff. I wasn't sure I needed to or wanted to.

"Won't Bas be a suspect too?" I asked him pushing the Christmas incident to the far corners of my mind.

"The police will want to talk to them both. Maybe Bas and Mavis will have solid alibis. Whit had been waiting a long time to date Mavis. Since all three went to LSU, Whit made no secret he always liked her," he said.

"They never dated?" I asked. "Ever?"

"No, not that I'm aware of," he said.

"So, Mavis files for divorce and it's clear sailing for Whit and Mavis to be together. Then he proposes to Justine, his law clerk? That had to make Mavis angry, if not homicidal. Was Whit using Mavis to one up Bas?"

"It seems that's been his life's mission. Whit was always all about Whit," he said. He looked at me and asked, "How come we both know all the same people and we didn't meet somewhere or at LSU earlier?" Jiff asked taking my hand.

"It would have been hard to meet you at LSU in Baton Rouge since I went to Loyola University here in New Orleans." I smiled. "Although I did spend a lot of time in Baton Rouge, I stayed in New Orleans mostly on weekends. There was always a party or something going on here. But, you are right, it is odd we didn't meet sooner."

"Exactly, and if, in theory, all people fall under six degrees of separation, New Orleanians must fall within two degrees, three at the most. I'd say the reason for that is all the socializing."

"There were so many bars, parties, and so little time," I said. "So, tell me about the Whit, Bas and Mavis love triangle."

"Mavis was crazy for Bas from the start. He was the big man on campus, Quarterback of the Tigers, and had a spot in the family law firm when he graduated. Bas got the girl while Whit got the girls. I always assumed Whit felt like he walked in Bas' shadow and worked hard to overcompensate for it."

"If Mavis didn't date Whit in college—she certainly recognized his personality well enough over the years—why would she do it now? It seems age has only rendered him a more exaggerated version of his younger self." I wondered aloud.

This made Jiff smile and say, "Which is not an improvement."

Hanky walked up to the both of us and speaking only to Jiff said, "You and Miss Alexander can leave. Taylor took her statement and one of us will contact you if I need to question her further."

Hanky was the only child raised by her cop dad so she lacked people skills and beauty knowledge. We had become friends when I had helped her with a makeover. Now men were checking her out instead of running away from her.

I was sure she was playing the professional card for Dante's sake. After all, Hanky started out as his partner and knew all the reasons we were no longer dating. She was a big advocate for me waiting for Dante telling me his case load would get more manageable once he was promoted to Captain. Really? Crime was only going up in New Orleans and Dante's case load would only get more manageable after he retired. I really didn't want to wait that long.

"Hanky, Justice is Whit's dog—a schnauzer he adopted from me—and he's missing," I said, ignoring her ignoring me. "I consider it important. Look at the paw prints. They are only bloody ones around the body. We should see bloody ones running away from the body. I'd say whoever did this took Justice with them."

"I'll look into it. Now you two leave…and Brandy…stay out of this," Hanky said. She did an eye roll toward Dante, adding in a lowered voice, "Call me if you find the dog."

Dante was actively ignoring us by feinting interest in a flower arrangement on the table at the other end of the hallway.

It was as good a time as any to speak to him. As I walked down the hall towards him, I could hear Hanky say to Jiff, "Oh, no, this isn't a good idea."

"Dante, that's a beautiful arrangement, isn't it?" I asked him and he looked up in surprise when I stood close to him.

"Yes, it is. I should have been bringing flowers like this to you," he said.

"Don't do that. We're good friends and I love you. I always will. We definitely weren't good together as a couple, and that's okay," I said. "Good friends are harder to come by so let's be good friends."

He nodded in agreement. "I've got a lot to deal with here with a dead judge in there—Whitmer of all people. It's gonna take a year to write down the list of suspects."

"And the list of wronged women he's dated," I said.

"I'd like to talk," he said never looking at me, only at the flowers. "Can I call you tomorrow?"

"Of course. We'll talk then." I turned to leave, and added, "Oh, the judge's dog is missing and you should look closely at the bloody paw prints around the body."

Chapter Five

A S SOON AS we were outside, I said to Jiff, "I know the neighbors across the street. Let's go ask the neighbors if they saw anything."

He guided me down the sidewalk to his car. Mine was still in the driveway blocked in by several police cars.

"You heard Hanky. She wants you to stay out of it," he said and opened the door for me to get in.

Before he could ask me what Dante and I talked about I said, "I'm trying to find Justice, the dog. I'm not interfering with the murder investigation," walking right past the car door Jiff held open for me. I added, "Whit, the neighbors' daughter, and I all attended the same grade school. We all used to hang out in high school."

Jiff let out a big breath and said my name, staccato-like, making it five syllables instead of two. "Brr. An. An. An. Dy." This was his way he said my name when he was exasperated. It made us both smile.

"I can talk to people I know," I said, sticking my nose in the air and picking up my pace so he had to hurry after me.

The Mouton home was directly across the street from Whit's, or rather, Whit's parents' home. Mr. Mouton was a banker and his daughter was in my freshman class in high school. She had married a banker-in-training. Her new husband worked for her dad. My school friend and her new hubby lived a few blocks away in the Garden District of the oh-so-desirable-area known as Uptown. The stately, grand homes, usually over a hundred years old, belonged to families for generations.

After Mrs. Mouton greeted me with a blank stare—she hadn't seen me in years—a giant smile crossed her face. A warm welcome to come in followed after I introduced myself. Even though she was French, she still spoke English with an accent.

"Brandy, it's been so long since we've seen you. Mon cher, come in, come in with your young man," she said standing aside. "Wait until Henry hears you are here." Raising her voice ever so slightly, she called for her husband to join her. She said his name the way the French pronounce it, OHN REE.

Mr. Mouton seemed to recognize me immediately and gave me a kiss on each cheek. New Orleanians kiss hello and goodbye, even with people we just met. The French tradition is to kiss on each cheek if you are acquainted with the person.

After I introduced Jiff to the Moutons I received an update on their daughter and her new husband. Mr.

Mouton asked me what the commotion was about across the street with all the police cars. This would be a shock to them and there was no easy way to deliver the news.

"I'm afraid I have bad news about your neighbor, Whit. He's dead, and it appears to be foul play," I said.

"Ooh-la-la! Murdered?" Mrs. Mouton asked as she put her hand over her heart, eyes wide while sinking into the chair behind her.

"Please sit," Mr. Mouton said. "Tell us what happened."

"Well, it's a little early in the investigation," Jiff said maintaining the lawyer's standard party line for not telling you anything. It was eerily similar to the police department's version of vagueness.

"I stopped by to return his suit coat that Whit left at Lancey's earlier this evening," I said. "Today was a landmark in his career when they voted him Best Judge of the Year in New Orleans. Whit resided over the much-publicized Clayton Haines case. It gained him notoriety. All his friends and colleagues were there to celebrate."

"Yes, I saw they voted him Best Judge of the Year in the paper," Mr. Mouton said taking a seat close to his wife on the settee.

"The gate and front door were open. I walked in and found him in his study."

"I'm sorry you had to be the one to find him," Mr. Mouton said. "His wife wasn't home?"

"You didn't know Whit and Claudette divorced again?" I asked.

"My, my," Mrs. Mouton said. "I thought I had seen Claudette over there this afternoon. I thought they were back together."

"Claudette was there when I arrived this afternoon. It seems she had business with Whit regarding their oldest son."

"Well, I'm not surprised they're divorced again. He didn't seem the type to settle down. We rarely see him since his parents died," Mr. Mouton said. "They were our friends, but the younger generation has their own set of friends. Whit gae his parents a lot to worry about. I would imagine the police will have no limit of suspects since he was a criminal judge," Mr. Mouton said.

"Mr. Mouton, did either of you see his dog, Justice, in the last couple of hours?" I asked. "It seems with the door and gate left open he may have escaped. I'd like to find him and take care of him until the police resolve this matter."

The Moutons looked at each other. Mrs. Mouton spoke first.

"Henry went to pick up our dinner we ordered. Neither of us wanted to go out or cook, but I don't remember hearing Justice barking and I didn't see him this evening." She looked at her husband and asked, "Henry, did you?"

Mr. Mouton said, "I didn't pay attention if the gate

or front door was ajar when I left and I didn't see or hear Justice. I haven't seen any dogs running off leash, or I would have remembered."

"Did you see any cars in the drive or parked out front?" I asked. I noticed in my peripheral vision Jiff turn his head and look at me.

"Come to think of it," Mr. Mouton said rubbing the side of his face as in deep thought, "I saw his executive assistant drive off in her Mercedes when I left to pick up dinner. Whit introduced us one day when she came to pick him up and I was waiting for a ride out on the sidewalk. She's a pretty lady with long dark hair. At first I thought it was Claudette."

"Do you remember what time you saw the car?" I asked.

He looked at his wife. Mrs. Mouton answered looking at Mr. Mouton as if conferring with him for approval before she said, "Seven o'clock, or a few minutes before. You asked what I wanted to order around six thirty and then left a few minutes after we decided and placed our order to go pick it up. I was working on some costume drawings for next year's Mardi Gras balls. You got back, and we sat down to eat at seven thirty-five. It usually takes about an hour from the time we decide what we want, order, pick it up and eat."

Mr. Mouton nodded in agreement as his wife spoke.

"Are you sure about the time you sat down to dinner?" I asked.

"Oh, yes. There's a mantle clock on the fireplace right behind Henry's head in the dining room. I see it every time I look at him," she said, smiling at her husband and putting a hand on his leg as he placed a hand over hers.

"Mr. Mouton, you didn't notice anyone or anything amiss when you returned with your dinner?" I asked.

"No, I'm sorry to say. Another Mercedes pulled up in the same spot Whit's assistant drove away from."

"Are you sure? Did you see the driver?"

"No, I backed out of our driveway and saw she was ready to pull away from the curb. I waved her to go ahead. When I drove off after her, that's when I saw the other car in my rearview mirror. By that time, I was almost to the corner. We rarely see Whit anymore so I got out of the habit of looking over there to wave hello like we did when his parents lived there," Mr. Mouton said.

"Could it have been Whit's assistant returning?" Jiff asked.

"No. I could still see her car about a block ahead of me and she drove straight a few more blocks and then turned. This was a different car," he said.

"Do you know whose car that was? Or did you see a man or woman get out?" I asked.

"No, sorry. I guess I'm not much good on behalf of our Neighborhood Watch Program." He stood up indicating he didn't have anything else to say on the subject of Whit's murder or he didn't want to. "Leave your number, Brandy and if we spot or catch Justice, I'll call you. He can't be far."

Jiff and I left after I gave them both a business card and kissed Mr. and Mrs. Mouton goodbye on each cheek. As we made our way to our cars, I noticed mine was still blocked in. We spotted Detectives Hanky and Travis leaving Whit's house, get into their unmarked police car and drive off in a hurry. Two uniform policemen started canvassing the neighbors on Whit's side of the street.

"Well, that's interesting," I said to Jiff as we arrived at his car nodding to my vehicle still hemmed in by multiple police vehicles with more arriving every minute. "It doesn't sound like Justine went inside. Maybe she just dropped him off? I wonder why? Were they arguing at Lancey's or could you tell?"

Jiff was deep in thought as he watched the two detectives drive away.

"Jiff, did you think Whit and Justine were not getting along earlier tonight?" I asked him again.

"No, I, uh, didn't get that they were arguing at the bar. She was right next to him. She's a hard one to read," Jiff said. He was distracted as he watched the unmarked car speed off.

I was about to ask him what was on his mind when his cellphone rang. He said, "It's Bas," he said to me as he answered. "Hey, what's up?" There was a pause, and he said, "Okay, I'll be right over. Don't say a thing."

"What happened?"

"Bas just got a call saying the police were on their way over to his home. They want to ask him about a phone call he made to Whit earlier this evening," Jiff said. "I've got to get over there. Do you need to get home or can you come with me?"

"I can go with you or I have to take an Uber home. My car's still blocked in," I said. "I wanted to look around for Justice but we can do that on the way over to Bas' house. They don't live far from here. Maybe I'll spot Justice along the way."

Chapter Six

WHILE WE DROVE over to the Martin home, I made a call into Whit's phone to see if I could access his voicemail messages. Claudette told me what she guessed was the voicemail code.

When the recording finished, I hit the pound sign, and the voice said, "Please enter your four-digit pass code to access your messages."

Yes! Whit was the poster boy for why it's a good reason to change your passwords and don't use the same one twice. He had the same one since; I don't know…forever. His answering machine looked like the first one ever made. I'm sure it was one his parent bought when they were alive. According to Claudette, I knew to enter 007, so I added a zero and made it 0007. Voila! Messages played from weeks ago. It would take me an hour to listen to them all. After the first one I listened to the tutorial on how to skip ahead by pressing the star sign so I did until I got to today's date.

"Jiff, you need to hear this," I said as he put the car in park. "It's the message Bas left Whit earlier this evening. The time stamp says it was while we were at

Lancey's." I enabled the speakerphone on my cell and hit replay. Bas' voice came over loud and clear.

There was no mistake or misunderstanding anything he said. 'You are the biggest narcissist I have ever had the misfortune to meet and to think I called you a friend. It wasn't bad enough to ruin Claudette's life twice, but you had to destroy everything in my life, Mavis's life and my daughter's. I will make you pay for the damage you did to all of us. You are dead to me.' That's the last message from today," I said.

"How did you get that?" Jiff sat behind the steering wheel holding it tightly, his hands in the ten and two o'clock positions like a student driver. He sat frozen in that position as he looked at me.

"Claudette told me his login probably hadn't changed, so I tried it. He used the same password for everything—the gate code, the security code, his voicemail access," I said adding, "since high school. Now that I think about it, the combination on his school locker in grade school was 007. He was a big Bond fan."

Jiff opened his eyes wider than I had ever seen. "You shouldn't be doing that. The police will charge you with tampering with evidence. I already have one client in this case. Are you trying to make it two?"

"I'm not tampering, changing or erasing anything. I'm only listening. Besides, by now," I said, "I'm sure the police listened to it and that's why Hanky and Travis took off running to Bas' house. See, that's their police unit parked in the driveway. From the ancient answering machine, I saw in Whit's office, you have to hit the replay button to listen to the messages."

"Yes, you say that like the police always have it so easy," he said smiling like his old self.

"It seems they are taking the easy way out. Why aren't they more concerned with Clayton Haines or the missing money?"

"I plan to ask them that very question," he said.

"I hoped we'd find Justice on the way," I said.

"Me too."

Jiff and I walked up to the stately Victorian Bas mansion on St. Charles Avenue near Napoleon. It had a side yard complete with a pool, gazebo, bathhouse and a four-car garage at the rear of the driveway on one side of the home. A gentleman wearing a black tuxedo opened the front door. He introduced himself as Mr. Walters and he let us in. He was very formal and asked if we were Miss Alexander and Mr. Heinkel. We nodded.

He asked if we would like something to drink. As much as I needed, correction…wanted a Rum and Tonic, I politely declined along with Jiff.

Mr. Walters informed us that Judge Martin and the New Orleans Police Officers waited for us in the parlor. We followed him to the room where everyone was waiting. When he opened the door to show us in he announced, "Miss Brandy Alexander and Mr. Heinkel, Esquire."

Bas, his fifteen-year-old daughter, Marigny, and the family dog, a big happy, but slobbering boxer were seated in the front parlor. Judge Bas sat on the red velvet Victorian sofa with one end in a wood that was carved in a high, back scrolled design, and the other in a low carved design. It was one of those sofas with an irregular height for the back. There was a small round marble-topped table next to him with a Waterford crystal decanter and matching Old Fashioned glasses on it. One of the Old Fashioned glasses was filled with whiskey. I caught a whiff of it from where I stood. Now, I was sorry I didn't ask for that drink.

Marigny sat opposite her father on a Victorian Chaise, or fainting couch, in matching red velvet.

There were other red velvet chairs with seats so close to the floor it required great control of your thighs least you plop into one and bounce off onto the floor. Large carved mirrors were over the fireplace mantles. There was a marble mantle by a fireplace on the living room end, and another one on the dining room end. The two rooms opened into each other that could be divided by ten-foot solid oak pocket doors that were now left open. The entire front of the house looked like the greeting room of a brothel. The dog sat on the floor on an Oriental carpet that matched the furniture design which was mostly red. Flaming red.

Since no one needed an introduction, the police started right in after taking a moment to look around at all the red. I'm sure they were thinking if there was blood in this room, it would be hard to notice.

"Ms. Alexander, could you please wait in another room," Hanky asked.

Great. Banished to the other room.

I nodded and smiled.

"Does my daughter have to be here?" Judge Bas asked. "She's been in her room studying since she got home from LSU today. And that was about 4:30 this afternoon."

Travis and Hanky looked at each other and agreed the girl could go back to her room.

Bas said, "Mr. Walters, please show Miss Alexander to the library."

Walters had been standing in the room, off to the side and invisible until Bas made the request.

Walters was a new addition to the Bas household or maybe he had been there and I visited so infrequently I didn't remember him. It seemed to me Walters must have used a cloaking device to render him invisible to the human eye until called upon to perform a service.

Marigny stood, and I noticed how tall she was. I also saw how much she looked like Mavis, only a younger version with her mother's classic good looks and poise. They could have been sisters. We followed Walters out.

In the center hallway I asked Walters to show me to the kitchen where I could wait.

"Judge Martin feels you would be much more comfortable in the library, Miss."

Besides his ability to cloak himself, Walters seemed to have the Jedi power of suggestion or mind control. I found myself saying, "Lead the way to the library."

I saw Marigny smile what seemed to be a nervous smile but thought kids that age don't want to be around adults or anyone not in their group. She followed us offering to show me where the newspapers and magazines were hidden. Marigny was a pretty girl, classy like the judge and as elegant a hostess as her mother, Mavis. Jiff had brought me to a party at their home right after we started dating.

"Are you at LSU already, Marigny? I didn't realize you had started college," I said noticing the LSU sweatshirt she wore.

"I'm at LSU in the gifted program. I tested in the upper percentile to start my education early. I'll start my premed curriculum at LSU next semester," she said.

"Are you driving now?" I asked. "Your dad mentioned you're fifteen. Isn't that when you get your learner's permit?"

"I have my learner's permit and I had a special dispensation to take Driver's Ed class this last semester."

I'm sure she did. I bet her Judge Daddy could get her any special dispensation she wanted. Too bad he didn't allow her to be her own age.

"That sounds exciting," I said. "Now you can bug your dad for a car."

"My dad ordered a new Mercedes and said I could

have his when the new one arrives," she said. Then she added, "My dad's been letting me practice on his car, the one I'm supposed to get. I don't see what the big deal is about driving. It's not that hard."

Marigny was correct. Driving was not that hard. Paying exclusive attention to operating a vehicle and not talking on a cellphone or texting was a more demanding discipline that did not involve the mechanics of driving.

She was an only child who belonged to the privileged class. It afforded her opportunities others worked their entire lives for. Her only contribution in life, to date, was that she was a member of the lucky sperm club.

Marigny had the additional benefit of her mother's pricey hairdresser and makeup consultant along with expensive clothes. She looked nineteen or twenty, exactly like Mavis in the photos I'd seen in the living room when Mavis was in college. She had a full figure at fifteen and she knew how to handle herself, I thought. Maybe it was bravado. She acted more mature than her age, but then, most teenagers now seem to.

Normally, she was quite composed but perhaps her dad being interrogated by the police had her nervous. She pulled at a strand of hair and twisted it around a finger. She wound it all the way to the top of her head, then untwisted it around the same finger in the other direction all the way out again. She repeated this one or two more times as we chatted and she showed me around the library.

After showing me to the newspapers money and investment magazines, she left me alone with my thoughts. I took a notepad and pen from my handbag to make notes of what had happened all evening so as not to forget a detail, large or small.

The first thing I wrote was Clayton Haines name with a question mark. I also wrote down all the details the Moutons told us with the times they recalled.

Jiff came to find me after about thirty minutes. He gave me his car keys and said to take his car to my house. He would be awhile, and he'd catch an Uber home when they were done. He walked me out to where his Mercedes was parked and gave me a kiss goodnight. It was like our first kiss at the parade where I walked up and kissed him in the middle of St. Charles Avenue for a handful of paper flowers. It was Mardi Gras, what can I say? Every kiss with him felt as if my clothes were melting off me.

When I realized I was standing in the street in front of the Martin home, still dressed, I cleared my throat to get his attention. He was caressing the side of my head with his hand when our intimate moment finally broke. I asked in a throaty, post-kiss sort of voice, "Why aren't the police more concerned with Clayton Haines? Doesn't it seem more than a coincidence that Whit gets murdered days after the jury found Haines guilty of first-degree murder in his court? That carries the death sentence for the biggest drug lord in the City of New

Orleans, doesn't it?" I asked him.

He took about a three-inch step back and said, "Yes, it carries the death penalty since a cop was killed. That's a question I'm going to ask them myself. Be careful and text me when you are safely home." He put his arm around me and guided me into the car door he opened. Then he handed me the key. As I drove off, I saw him in the rear view mirror. He stood in the street and watched me drive away.

Chapter Seven

L AST NIGHT I left the Martin home at 11:00 p.m. Luckily, today was Saturday and I could sleep in, meaning I might get a chance to stay in bed as long as Meaux wanted to. Meaux, my little black schnauzer, had a built-in alarm set for 6:00 a.m. sharp every morning. Sometimes I managed to get him to stay a few more minutes if I scratched him while I was half awake. Today, I had to find Justice, and Meaux did his part by getting me up and onto that job.

The whole Whit murder bothered me. I should have been better friends with Claudette since we attended school together, but we never did anything outside of school, such as go over to each other's house. I knew Whit from grammar school and he teased me every day since I was the tallest girl in our school. He was the tallest boy and his drawing attention to me only made me feel self-conscious. I learned to roll with it. In high school, I often saw Whit at my high school dances since he dated Suzanne—my best friend in high school then, and my roommate now.

That was before Claudette set her sights on him.

Claudette made no secret she was crazy for Whit. I never dated him but had been on several double dates with girlfriends who did. I liked Whit's company in a group. I found him charming and entertaining but I didn't want to be the girl who had to put up with him at the end of the evening. Whit and I never had a friendly, one-on-one conversations. Our friendship had been casual from a distance, but I liked him. To date him was not to like him—I had heard that often enough from girls left in his dating wake.

There were so many inconsistencies popping in my head, I had written them down while waiting in the Martin home library last night. The biggest one that nagged me was why would a killer, sent by Clayton Haines, take the dog? If it was Haines, why wasn't there evidence of a break-in? Would Whit just open the door to one of his gang who all looked like they spent time in the Central Lockup Do-It-Yourself Tattoo Parlor? Why wasn't Justice in the kitchen behind the gate? Whit usually put him there to keep him out of the way if someone came over that Justice didn't know.

I got a text from Jiff asking if I wanted to meet him early for a cup of coffee. It was 7:00 a.m. and he wanted to Uber to the City Park beignet and coffee shop and have me meet him with his car. He wanted to tell me what happened with Hanky, Travis and Bas. I texted him back *That's perfect.*

I loved sitting outside in City Park having a morning cup. It served the best brewed coffee and chicory in the world, according to me. It was a romantic spot as well in an old mission-style building that had been selling refreshments since the 1913's. It was nestled under giant oak trees next to the lagoon with ducks quacking for a beignet handout. The other plus was it stayed open twenty-four hours a day, and not only had the best, but also, the least expensive cup of coffee in New Orleans.

I texted back, *I'll be there in about thirty minutes. Are you bringing Isabella? If so, I'll bring Meaux.*

Isabella was a schnauzer and Jiff's dog. Meaux and Isabella hadn't been on a playdate together in a while. I added to my text, *Let's walk them around the pond after we have our coffee, or take them to the dog park.*

Bring him, Jiff texted back.

Meaux and Isabella shared an order of three beignets. It kept them content to sit like statues in the chairs between us waiting for a piece of the powdered sugar donut treat. The waiters brought water for our dogs and steaming café au lait for us. Until we completed a ritual of sip coffee, break a piece of beignet for each fuzzy face until gone, we couldn't exchange information over the events of last night.

Once I gave Meaux the all gone signal he was content to sit in the chair and wait until we finished talking. The all gone signal I used with him was the move blackjack dealers did when leaving a gaming table—palms up, palms down, then scissoring hands to show no cards were held. Once I did this, he stopped begging.

"Tell me why the police are so interested in Bas," I said.

"Well, for starters, they wanted to talk about the message on the answering machine you so skillfully hacked. I argued that a heated phone message left from across town is not proof of wrongdoing," he said. "But they wanted a rundown on the affair Mavis had with Whit resulting in their two divorces."

"What did the police say about Clayton Haines? Anything?" I asked.

"No, apparently they were more interested in a police report made by the restaurant manager the night the six of us were all at the restaurant in Canal Place a few months ago. Whit and Bas got into that fist fight over the champagne delivered to the table, remember?"

"How could I forget? When it arrived, Whit commented that champagne was Mavis's favorite," I said.

"Bas' antennae went up. He took issue with Whit knowing it was Mavis's favorite since he thought that special brand was only shared by he and his wife for, how shall we say...special moments." Jiff said.

"I think it would have blown over if Claudette hadn't flown into a rage when she realized the implications Bas was alluding to right before he punched Whit," I said. "It was a nice evening up to that point."

"You know, I asked Whit about ordering that. He said he didn't and I know Bas didn't. If I had ordered champagne, it would have been your favorite. It wasn't on the bill either. Someone had paid for it anonymously," Jiff said as he seemed to ponder.

"It had to be someone who knew we would all be there. Whoever it was had access to personal info about Whit and Mavis. Anyone come to mind, like a secretary, law clerk or the next girlfriend in the Whit lineup?" I asked.

"Justine." Jiff said her name and didn't even seem surprised.

"That's who I'd put my money on," I said. "And, I bet Whit had already started sniffing around Justine. Claudette told me Mavis filed for divorce shortly after that. First, the incident in the restaurant, then Bas caught Mavis with Whit coming out of the elevator at the Fairmont."

"Mavis filed for divorce?" Jiff asked surprised.

"That's what Claudette said. Bas called to tell her so she wasn't blindsided. She had already left Whit for the second time over the champagne incident. It crushed Claudette that Mavis was having an affair with Whit. They'd been friends as couples, good friends Claudette thought, since college, maybe even high school."

Jiff waved the server over and paid our bill. The dogs were ready to move and came alive as soon as we stood. We started off walking at a good clip. The giant pond near the café and beignet stand was a close walk to take the dogs on. I needed to relax, and walking helped to clear my head so I could make sense of the facts and information assaulting me.

We walked over the hump in a small bridge by the lagoon and past the New Orleans Museum of Art. At the front of the museum we could look up a double drive entrance with a wide neutral ground to lovely Esplanade Avenue. A large lagoon sat opposite the museum with a walking/biking path. The area had a general relaxing pastoral feel.

The giant pond offered numerous rentals for your City Park experience—bicycles, gondolas, or surrey cycles for two- to four people. We passed an area near the café and beignet shop that rented paddle boats. If we didn't have the dogs, I would have suggested renting a paddle boat. Something about cruising over the water always relaxed me and helped me clear my head.

"Why would Mavis give up everything with Bas to have an affair with Whit? He hounded her in college to date and she only had eyes for Bas. It seems if she didn't see what kind of character he was back then, given youthful naiveté, she must have seen his stripes over the years," Jiff said.

"Maybe she was bored in her marriage," I said. "So, the police want to hang this on Judge Martin? That should be a political hot potato for Captain Deedler and his Commissioner."

"Always concerned for Dante?" Jiff said and smiled.

"It's not that, or him for that matter. Any cop, in that job, with this case will get an ulcer over it," I said trying to coax Meaux to walk in the same direction as Isabella. "Let's go walk them around the pond. Moving around helps me think better."

"The police seem to be stuck on Bas as the murderer and while he may have legitimate issues with Whit, I can't see Bas doing it," Jiff said.

"I can't either," I said.

We opted to walk the pedestrian side of the bike path around the lagoon. Joggers passed us. Sometimes the dogs would bark but most of the time they were more interested in sniffing the closest bush, bench or trash can on our route.

"Although crimes of passion seem to far outweigh other good old random crimes. Murder for money is a close second. The police put a higher value on investigating those knowing the victim verses those who might be more random. This however, doesn't feel random," Jiff said.

"What caused his death? I didn't touch anything but I saw a lot of blood under him around his knees and elbows. Was he shot or stabbed?" I asked.

"Well, it appeared someone shot him multiple times with a small caliber weapon. One that didn't kill him right away. We won't know how many or with what until the coroner submits a report," Jiff said.

"OMG," I said making a face thinking of the noise. "Multiple times? How come no one heard it? None of the neighbors heard shots? The front door was open for goodness sake. I get a dozen texts from my Good Neighbor app if a car in the neighborhood backfires, all asking if anyone heard a gunshot."

"The door might have been left open when the murderer left but stayed closed while he was inside with Whit. Using a pillow or a small caliber could have muffled the sound. That's most likely the reason no one heard it. Someone wanted something from Whit," Jiff said. "A small caliber allows the shooter to do a lot of damage without killing the victim immediately."

"Yes, although many facts are not adding up. It had to be someone his dog, Justice, recognized if Whit didn't put him behind the kitchen gate," I said.

"You're forgetting Whit had a few drinks at Lancey's, and possibly one or two more after he got home," Jiff said.

"If Justice was behind the gate, Justice had access via a doggie door to the backyard. He could have escaped the unlocked iron gate but the bloody paw prints suggested he was there when Whit was murdered. It must have been someone who knew about the safe, that he kept money in it and knew the security code to get into the home," I said.

"Well, half the city of New Orleans knows the security code and now one more knows the voicemail password." He eyed me as we walked along and stopped at every shrub.

"This is really a stop and sniff, not a walk," I said. "For every five steps we take, one of them, mostly Meaux, has to stop and sniff something. C'mon Meaux, how are we going to get any exercise like this?"

"The problem is there's no shortage of suspects,"

Jiff said.

"Right. Let's see, there's Bas and Mavis Martin, Justine whom no one has heard from, and the Clayton Haines entire army of soldiers. There might be someone Whit owed money to...besides Claudette. Then, let's not forget the laundry list of criminals Whit has sentenced and thrown in jail. Claudette, the ex-wife, who married him twice, and had twice the reason for wanting him dead. I'm sure there's no limit to the number of people who remembered Claudette often said she would kill him," I said. "I've heard it many times myself."

Jiff said. "That list of suspects is longer than people in line at Randazzo's ordering King Cakes at Mardi Gras," Jiff said. "You left out the women he dated and wronged."

"It's time we talk to Justine," I said. "And Mavis Martin."

"Bas told me where Mavis is living, and you will never guess," Jiff said laughing.

I raised my eyebrows asking the silent question.

He answered, "Julia's bed and breakfast."

Chapter Eight

"**D**ROP ME AT my car after we see Justine," I said. "I'll go to Julia's under the pretense of visiting my friends and if Mavis is there, I'll chat her up."

"You know who will have the most info on Mavis, right?" Jiff asked.

We both answered at the same time. "Frank."

Frank was the concierge, receptionist, groundskeeper, Boy Friday, Seamstress, Interior Designer...the all-around slave to Julia's every whim who worked for her at the guest house/hotel she owned.

"Do you want to take the dogs with us?" Jiff asked.

"Sure, why not? Justine should like dogs, after all, Whit had Justice," I said. "Julia likes dogs. What's one more in that pack of curs she has out back?"

Justine wasn't home. If she was, she wasn't answering the door of her French Quarter apartment. I hit the door buzzer for the apartment next in number to hers and someone answered.

"Justine?" I asked.

"No, she's in 105," a man answered.

"Oh, I'm sorry. I must have hit the wrong button

the second time. She was supposed to be home, and she didn't answer," I said. I stuck my tongue out at Jiff when he made a disapproving face indicating he knew I was playing this guy and hoping for some info.

"I haven't heard her leave or any noise from her apartment today," he said. "I'm sure she's not home."

He signed off before I could say thanks.

"We could sit outside at that café up the street and have coffee," Jiff said. "Maybe she'll return before we're ready to leave."

"That's a grand idea," I said.

Two whining dogs and two cups of coffee later, still no Justine.

"I've had enough caffeine for one day," I said.

"We'll have to catch her another time. During the week might be easier since she'll be at Whit's office getting things in order," Jiff said.

Then it hit us. That's where she is now—Whit's office!

We drove to the courthouse and there was Whit's car in his reserved parking space marked, Judge Whitmer. There was no sign of Justine's car in the visitor spots or on the street. We decided to try to catch her Monday morning when court would be in session. Jiff said she should be there to help reschedule Whit's calendar moving his cases to other judges.

"Well, it's odd that Whit's car is still parked here," I said.

"I'm sure he leaves his car here lots of times and

makes her drive him," Jiff said.

🐐 🐐 🐐 🐐 🐐 🐐 🐐 🐐 🐐 🐐

WHEN I WAS heading to Julia's Canal Street Guest House, I got a call from Amy, the West Bank Animal Shelter manager that probably has my cell number on speed dial whenever a schnauzer comes in.

"Hey, Amy," I answered.

"Brandy, someone tied a little schnauzer to the gate. He was here this morning when we opened. When I checked the microchip on him, it shows your rescue pulled him from the shelter four years ago. I'd put him on a stray hold until the owner comes to claim him, but we're slammed full of dogs. Can you come get him and talk to the person you adopted him to?"

"Yes, but tell me something. Does that dog have Neuticles?" I had a feeling it was Whit's dog.

"Yes, how did you know?" she said.

Neuticles were what owners, mostly men, had surgically implanted in their male pets after the dog is neutered to represent testicles that normally shrink and disappear in about six months.

"I know who that dog belongs to," I said. "And as much as I'd like to talk to him, I can't. The guy was murdered last night, and that dog went missing. I'll be right there to pick him up," I said.

Whit had Neuticles implanted on Justice after he adopted him from me. I was so angry with him I didn't speak to him for a month, not that he noticed.

"Oh, wow, sorry about the owner, but I'm glad this little dude wasn't hurt. He'll be in my office, away from the general population when you get here. Whoever tied him to the fence, tied him in a puddle of water, so bring a towel. He's still a muddy mess," she said. "Oh, and he had another tag on him in addition to the microchip tag, his rabies tag and your rescue tag. I don't recognize this other tag but one of the shelter workers said it's something new to track and find your dog. There was nothing with an owner's name, only yours."

"Amy, did he have any blood on him?" I asked.

"None that I saw. The shelter worker who found him when they came to work this morning assumed he was injured. The puddle of water he was sitting in was red with what she thought was blood. Our vet gave him a once over and she didn't find any injuries on him," she said. "I gotta run."

"Thanks, Amy, I'm on my way." Making a house call at Julia's Bed and Breakfast would have to wait.

🐐 🐐 🐐 🐐 🐐 🐐 🐐 🐐 🐐

THE INFORMATION DESK attendant at the shelter instructed me to go through the doors to the adoption area to find Amy. Every time someone walked through the doors to the dogs adoption area, all the dogs barked. I swear it was each one saying, "Come look at me, I'm a good dog to go home with."

As soon as someone walked close to their run, they

stopped barking, wagged their tails, and sat calmly at the fenced gate. They waited for someone to open it, look them over, approve and take them home. Each one was putting their best paw forward hoping for a fur-ever home. It broke my heart. I glanced over of all the runs to make sure there wasn't another schnauzer hiding out.

"Hey Brandy!" Amy yelled over the barking. She waved at me to follow her. Once we were out of the adoption area it was quiet and we could talk.

"Are those soundproof doors?" I asked.

"You would think so, but they stop barking when there's no one in there to notice them." Amy and I shared a sorrowful look.

When we got to Amy's office, there was Justice sitting in her chair looking at the computer screen like he was trying to decide what app to use.

"He made himself right at home," Amy said smiling.

"Hey, Justice. Remember me?" I said and knelt down to the floor.

Justice jumped down from Amy's chair and ran over to me wagging his tail.

He had come to me in rescue because he was bred to be a stud at a breeder's puppy mill. However, Justice showed no interest in female dogs so, they tried to sell him. I found he was for sale on a local internet site I have set up to send me alerts for schnauzers for resale or re-homing. The breeder wanted one hundred dollars for him.

I bought him, then had rescue vet him. He was neutered, given all shots, vaccines and a microchip. He was a beautiful little dog, black and silver. Whit loved him at first sight until I told him his testicles would shrink up and disappear in about six months.

He had asked, "Why did you do that to my dog?"

I answered, "Because in rescue we want to stop, not add to the overpopulation of unwanted pets. Neutering or spaying rescues is one thing we do not negotiate on. You are welcome to go buy your own dog from some breeder."

After he saw Justice he said, "No, I want this little guy. He is perfect for me and his name will be Justice."

I had thought the name was fitting and had no idea Whit, the big goof, would have Neuticles implanted for Justice. Why do men consider their dog's testicles, or lack thereof, a reflection of their own manhood? I never told him what the breeder said. If Whit had been aware that Justice showed no interest in his female canines, he might have given him testosterone shots or Viagra. Personally, I figured Justice had not found the right girl schnauzer. He was selective, unlike his owner.

"Brandy, today being Saturday, we have a lot of people in looking to adopt. I gotta get back to work," Amy said.

"Sure, sorry to take up so much of your time. Thanks for calling me and putting him in solitary until I got here. Hope you get them all adopted today!" I said and left with Justice while Amy headed back to the adoption area.

🐐 🐐 🐐 🐐 🐐 🐐 🐐 🐐 🐐 🐐

I LEFT THE shelter and drove straight to the grooming salon my friend, Jill, owns. She gets the rescues cleaned up and presentable for me. She had a full house of dogs there to bathe, groom and board, but she made room for Justice.

"I think he only needs a bath. A shelter worker found him in a muddy puddle tied to a fence. He's not injured, but if you find any blood on him, cut or shave it off and put it in an envelope or plastic bag for me. It might be evidence."

"Sure, I'll do that," Jill said giving Justice the once over. "We'll get him fixed up," she said.

"Have you ever seen or heard of one of these on his collar? The tag says Find Me. Do you know if it's an app or GPS locator or something?"

Jill studied the tag. It looked like a rabies tag or microchip tag and just said FindMe.com. "I haven't seen this one in particular, but I've heard there's a new tracker, like a GPS chip they are putting in dogs or on their collars. That's all I know," she said. Then she gave Justice a head rub, picked him up and said, "If he needs a touchup we'll get him looking handsome. Come back around six. He should be ready then."

I thanked Jill and texted Jiff. *The SPCA called me with a dog and it was Justice. He's getting groomed right now.* Then my phone rang.

"The dog might be evidence," he said when I answered. "You need to call Hanky or, or, or that other detective. What's his name?"

"You mean Taylor, that other detective?" I asked. I figured he wasn't suggesting I call Dante. "If I give the police the dog, they'll treat him like evidence and quarantine him at the SPCA. That's where all the pit bulls are waiting to go to court on bite cases. He could be there months in a loud, noisy and stressful environment. You know how long a murder trial can take just to get it scheduled on the docket. Add to that all the postponements, rescheduling or delays, then continued, blah, blah, blah."

"Yes, but," he started to say.

"No but. That dog is still registered to me as the owner who adopted him from the shelter and I went to claim him. Period. Paragraph. End of story."

"Well, okay. I suggest you tell Hanky or Taylor about him. See what they want you should do," Jiff said in his agreeable, charming way of getting me to do things I really didn't want to do. I could almost hear him smile on the other end of the line. He was too nice and well intentioned for me not to see it his way.

"OK, I might ask them if they need the dog…should I find him." I said. "I'm on my way to see Julia right after I drop Meaux home."

"Dinner tonight? How about sitting outside at Santa Fe? The cold front came through and it will be a beautiful evening, and besides, I love the food there."

"Yes, there's a real chill in the air now since it dropped from one-hundred degrees to ninety. You're right, the weather today is a lot more pleasant with a lot less humidity. I can be ready after 6:30 p.m.," I said.

"I'll pick you up then. Love you," Jiff said and hung up.

Chapter Nine

I SAT IN my car in front of Jill's Pet Parlor ready to leave when my phone rang and when I looked at it; it had to be Dante. There was no number on Caller ID, only PRIVATE.

He didn't say hello or any of the pleasantries when calling someone. He launched a question as soon as I hit answer.

"Did you already have lunch?" he asked.

"Hello Dante," I said. Some things never change like his dismal phone etiquette. My biggest pet peeve is he hangs up without saying goodbye. The only way to know a call with him has ended is when you hear the dial tone.

"Lunch, have you eaten yet?" he repeated.

"No."

He suggested we meet at Central Grocery on Decatur. I agreed and asked myself when was the last time I had the best Muffuletta in the city? Actually, I considered Central Grocery's the only Muffuletta in the city. Everyone else made a distant second.

Central Grocery originated this giant gastric delight

stuffed with ham, salami, provolone and their signature olive salad. Their crusty Sicilian sesame bread is nine-inches round and looks as big as a pizza pan. It's huge and I didn't care about any diet today. Since I'm a nervous eater and King Cakes are my go to comfort food, Central Grocery's big, awesome Muffuletta would do the trick to satisfy my nervous needs if I had to deal with Dante.

Keeping our conversation in a public place seemed more appropriate if there was the slightest chance he would get all maudlin over the proposal thing that happened. It was my family's opinion it was the disaster of the century. I thought it worked out the best for me given all the other ways it could have gone. There are members of my family I'm still not speaking to over it.

I took Meaux back into Pet Parlor and asked if she would let him stay for a play date in the small dog area until I came back for Justice. She said yes, and Meaux ran off all excited to sniff and greet new friends. I call it the doggie handshake.

When I got to Central Grocery Dante was inside at a bar height table having a beer. There was a cup of coffee on the table for me.

"Are you off duty?" I asked looking from him to the beer.

"Yeah, if I get called for a homicide I can send Hanky and Taylor," he said pulling out the bar stool for me to sit on.

Uh oh. This sounded like the talk on how his life,

work…everything has changed, now he's in more control with scheduled time off. This was the age-old argument I maintained when we were sort of dating. I say 'sort of dating' because we never completed a date after we left high school. Dante joined the military after high school and when he returned, he joined the New Orleans Police Department working homicide. We'd start out with dinner or a movie, and he'd get a call and off to a dead body he went. Most of the time, I had to taxi or find a way home alone. It always made me wonder why he was in such a hurry to get to a dead body that wasn't moving or going anywhere.

"You hungry?" he asked.

"I might eat a quarter of a Muffuletta. Wanna split one? You can have three-fourths," I said.

"That's fine." He waved over the gal who had been watching us when I walked in and ordered.

Meeting Dante in the French Quarter in the middle of the day was as good as being on a desert island. No one, and I mean no one, wanted to come to the French Quarter and park for a lunch meeting. Locals who worked the Quarter came here to eat, but today, Saturday, we were surrounded by tourists.

We didn't need a menu to order.

There was the awkward start up conversation with exchanging the status on everybody, his parents, my parents, his brothers, including the one who married my sister. I asked how his job was going with his new promotion to keep him talking in the ozone layer and not make the conversation personal—to him and I. However, that was the wrong question for me to ask him.

"That's what I wanted to talk to you about," he said staring at his beer.

Uh oh.

"Can you tell me anything about what's going on with Whit? Any suspects?" I asked trying to derail what was coming.

"You know I can't talk about an ongoing investigation," he said.

"Right, but did you even look at the paw prints around the body? They didn't run off. That might mean whoever took the dog might be who killed Whit," I said. Then I realized I had the dog. I pondered if I should tell him.

"I'm pretty sure the killer isn't worried about animal rescue," Dante said. "I don't want to talk about that murder, crime, whatever. I want to talk about us."

"Wait just a minute before we talk about us," I said at the exact moment I reached across the table and put my hand on his arm that our sandwich arrived.

"Here y'all go, Dante," she said, her eyes darting to Dante, my hand on his arm and then back to his face. "One Muffuletta and two plates. Enjoy."

The waitress knew his name so he must come here often to eat, drink beer or maybe to talk to her. She was a pretty girl and I noticed there was interest or a spark there for him.

"Justice has some kind of tracker implanted in him that might lead him to the killer," I said. "Not a microchip to give the owner's name, but a chip like a GPS locater to find him. The program tracks everywhere the dog went."

"And why is this important to this investigation?" he asked.

"Because it should track where Justice went after he left Whit's house. Remember, the bloody paw prints that didn't run away from the body? I think someone who knew and liked the dog picked him up and took him with them."

"Why? Why kill someone and not leave their dog?"

"I believe they took him because of the barking. The dog barking or running after them barking might bring attention sooner than later to the body," I said. "That's my opinion."

"Good to know, Detective Alexander," he said placing the plates next to the sandwich so he could divide it.

"I hope you choke on your Muffuletta. I'm trying to help you," I said.

"You find the dog and I'll find the killer, how's that?" he said.

"I believe the dog will lead you to the killer. Just think about it," I said.

"Why take the dog? Why not leave him in a closet or kill the dog too? I'm glad the killer didn't, but why take the dog?"

"Perhaps the killer wanted a pet for their kid, what can I say? People are strange." He started on the sandwich after plopping a quarter of it onto the second plate and sliding it across the table to me.

And here I was sitting across from Dante, one of the strangest people I knew.

I figured we wouldn't get back to the subject of our dating/proposal/break-up situation until after we ate. After he finished one of his three quarters of our shared Muffuletta, he wiped his mouth, put down the napkin. "I know we sort of left off on the wrong foot on Christmas Eve when Hanky busted in and pulled me off to the Clayton Haines murders remember?"

How could I forget?

"Yes, I remember. I wouldn't call it leaving off on the wrong foot. That's all behind us, let's move on," I said trying to avoid reliving that train wreck.

"Well, it might have been a mistake getting Woozie and your Dad involved tricking you into showing up. You didn't think I'd be back in town until after Christmas, but I wanted to surprise you."

"It was more like a shock treatment than a surprise. If you remember, we hadn't seen or talked to each other in a few months," I said trying to cut him off before he launched into a spiel he obviously prepared.

"Oh, right," he said. The waitress was hovering around the empty table next to us wiping off the top which was already clean. "That's because I was just promoted and it was overwhelming at first. I didn't realize so much time was passing."

"Before you say anything else, I need to tell you our moment has come and gone, and I don't mean Christmas. That moment happened before the holiday." I realized I might live to regret the next thing I wanted to say. "I'll always love you Dante, but our relationship was never even close to normal. I want and have normal now." Men hear what they want to and I really hoped he didn't lock onto "I'll always love you, Dante…"

"No, you have Richie Rich now," he said. He turned and motioned to our waitress for the check.

"Richie Rich? Do you mean Jiff?"

"Yes. I did a background check on him and his whole family. His parents, his brothers, their wives or girlfriends and his grandmother."

"What? You did what?" I almost choked on a bite of Muffuletta I tried to swallow fast. I was absolutely flabbergasted and wanted to box him upside his head. After a couple of stunned moments of silence, where my thoughts were spinning around like they were inside the funnel of a tornado, I stuttered, "Why? What did you find want to find out about them?"

"Well, there was nothing really. I was hoping to find out they all practiced animal sacrifice or had puppy mills. I figured that's the only thing that would turn you off about them. For me, I was hoping they had mob ties or multiple arrests for drugs, something like that so I could throw them all in jail."

"That would make you happy?" I asked not believing what he said.

"Yes, but they're all pillars of the community. I couldn't find one unpaid parking ticket. Do you know how boring those people are? It must be all that money they have that keeps you interested," he said looking down into his lap.

He looked so disappointed in himself that it was hard not to feel sorry for him.

"I can't believe you ran a background check on all of them. His parents have money the grandmother left them, not Jiff or his brothers. Jiff has a job he works at every day, just like you and me," I said trying to keep the irritation out of my voice. I wanted to be grateful, but I realized he didn't do it to protect me or because he was worried about me. He did it to send a wrecking ball into my relationship with Jiff. "I'm sure you found out they are very nice, normal people."

"That's just it. With my promotion, I have more time and can send other detectives out when I used to have to go. My life is getting more normal, just like you wanted."

"You really think the late night, spur-of-the-moment murders will stop and give you a normal life now that you are the Captain?"

"No, not completely. I work for the police department, remember? Hanky is my right hand now. She deals with everything like I used to. She's more than capable. She handles everything, and she only calls me if it is warranted, like the Judge last night." He reached across the table and held out his hand for me to take it.

The waitress wiping off the next table knocked the metal napkin dispenser onto the floor which made us both jump and look at her. Dante had pulled his hand back when he heard the noise which had a pop like a small caliber handgun.

"Maybe there won't be as many high-profile cases like the judge last night, but criminals go to work every Christmas, every New Year, and every holiday. That makes them a high-profile case because the media keeps it in front of the public until it's solved. That means, you're pulled into it until it's solved. Don't you see? It's not going to change. If anything, crimes and murders are on the rise."

The waitress brought the check. Dante paid, and on the way out the door asked if we could walk round Jackson Square a few minutes. I looked at my watch and it was only 2:30 p.m.

"Sure. It's only a block and I'm parked in that direction," I said.

A group of high school kids with instruments were practicing at the entry gate into Jackson Square. It looked like some band members were contemplating making music a career. They had their instrument cases open for tips. Dante and I each put in a dollar. They played so loud and terrible we walked to the far side of Jackson Square near the Cathedral just so we could hear each other talk.

"I still visit your dad if the light's on in the garage. You should call him. He feels bad things turned out like they did at Christmas, with…well…you know. He thinks you'll never speak to him again."

"He knows better. That would mean I'd be forcing him to be the only person who has to listen to my mother, and that's cruel and unusual punishment," I said. "I just don't want to go over there and have to listen to my mother on how I'm the big bad guy in all of it. She'll blame me. You live next door, that's at least two walls and an ally separating you from her," I said.

"No, I don't live at my parents' home anymore. I moved out about two months ago. It was too much seeing them look at me with pitiful stares all the time. I like to stop and visit your dad though."

"Well, he's the one whose closest to normal in my family," I said and we both laughed. "Where did you move to?"

"I'm in the Carrollton-Riverbend area. I'd like you to come see the place I'm renting. It needs a little help in the decorating department," he said. "Maybe you could make some suggestions."

"I'd like that," I said looking at my watch. Before he could ask me to go there today—like now—I added, "I need to get going, but call me next week and let's plan a time for me to visit. I'd love to see your place. Any suggestions I make and you don't use, will not hurt my feelings."

"That would be great. I'm walking distance to

several places to eat. Maybe you can come see it next week and I'll take you to dinner."

I smiled and stood up to leave. This was the first time we had had a conversation from beginning to end without a call from homicide interrupting us. It was also the first time we had had a conversation that didn't involve Dante telling me to stay out of one of his investigations.

I gave him a hug, and he hugged me back. Neither of us said goodbye but I felt him watching me as I walked back to where I parked.

Chapter Ten

FRANK OPENED THE double-leaded glass doors of Julia's Bed and Breakfast as I made my walk up the front steps. He was wearing wide-legged, black, palazzo pants that looked more like a skirt, a red silk blouse with silk-covered buttons up the back and his signature kitten pumps...black. He had grown his hair out a little longer from the pixie cut which now looked like a pageboy. Frank also wore enough black eyeliner to make him look like a member of a heavy metal band.

"Well, I'd announce your arrival miss, but I don't think I can recall your name. It's been forever since you were last here," Frank said with his head held high, hands on his hips with an attitude of southern pretentiousness becoming Scarlett O'Hara.

"Maybe I should leave and come back when you can recall who I am," I said in my best southern accent which was far from good. I'm a New Orleanian. I speak New Orleanian. So does Frank.

"Come here, you big silly and give me a hug," he said. "I'll go fetch her highness. She's planning a coronation, a ball or a beheading...something that has slipped my mind because of its unimportance."

Frank was referring to my friend, Julia, who owned the guest house.

"Wait, Frank. I need to ask you something. Can we talk a minute, someplace quiet?" I asked looking around for a suitable corner where we wouldn't be in the middle of the entry hall.

"If it's about the Queen, she hears all. I think she's bugged all the rooms," he said in a loud whisper.

"No, not her. One of your guests," I said talking through one of my forced smiles showing all my teeth.

Frank nodded and crooked his index finger, signaling for me to follow him.

He opened a door that was about five feet high under the staircase which did not have a hall bath in it but was a storage closet. It was a fairly large closet that two people could easily stand up in after they ducked through the doorway. I had first hand knowledge because he pulled me into it with him.

"Are you trying to tell me you're still in the closet?" I asked him.

Frank answered me by shaking his head no, rolling his eyes while he fluttered a hand as if he was batting away a mosquito to dismiss my remark. He did however, let a smile squeeze from his lips.

"It's a cedar closet, so it's double insulated with wood. She had me test it with her but I cheated. I told her I couldn't hear her even when she screamed. I lied. I could. Then I didn't say anything when she pushed me in here and said to talk normally. I started to talking normally when she opened the door."

By she, he meant Julia.

"So, Julia and everyone can hear us?" I asked.

"If you whisper or speak softly, she won't. I tested that with her to make sure. I said she was a fat cow and would never get a man. She didn't beat me about the head and shoulders when she opened the door so it's safe to say she didn't hear me."

"Frank, you risk your life and take more chances than Black Op Agents," I said. "Julia has ways of making you talk."

"I've have escape plans in place. I'll get out before she closes in on me," he said.

"What kind of escape plans?" I asked. This might be good.

"Well, I bought a wig exactly like Gloria's. It was cheap. Gloria really should invest in a better-quality wig, I mean, after all it is her appearance," he said.

"Escape plans, Frank. Stay focused," I said.

"I keep the wig in here along with one of Gloria's uniforms. They are so starched they can stand up by themselves so I look like her when I put it on with the wig. Then, I roll up my pants and I walk out the front or side door. What else do you need to know?"

"That's genius, Frank. I'd love to see you in that disguise. Julia doesn't get suspicious if she sees Gloria upstairs one minute, then going out the front door?" I asked.

"The Queen doesn't pay that much attention to her subjects. She'll think Gloria is putting out the trash or getting the mail—work stuff," he said.

"How do you get out of here if Gloria isn't working? What else do you do to get out of here unnoticed?" I asked. This was so much fun I didn't want it to end. "Your secrets are safe with me."

Frank pointed to the floor.

"Are you digging a tunnel?" I asked.

"No, silly." He bent down and peeled the carpet away from the corner of the closet floor revealing a trap door.

"If the wig and uniform disguise is too dangerous, then I slip out this way. I already put one of those blue plastic drop cloths left over from Katrina under there so I won't get all muddy if it's a rainy day."

"Julia doesn't know about this hatch?"

"No, and you better not tell her. I found it when she asked me to tidy up this closet and replace the old carpet in here. Good for me, bad for her."

"This will be our little secret. Now, Mavis Martin. What can you tell me about her?" I said in my best secret agent imitation.

Frank glanced around the cedar closet before he answered. "She was recently divorced from her husband—a judge—and she planned to run off with another judge—the husband's best friend. When the second judge, whom we will refer to as The Cad Judge, took up with a pretty young thing working for him.

Also, there's some conjecture floating about that The Cad Judge, not the husband Judge, had some serious porn and gambling issues. Mavis, we will call the woman who makes poor decisions by that name..."

"That's because it is her name," I said.

Frank waved his hand in the air to dismiss what I said.

"She, the woman known as Mavis, worried about her daughter and had gotten bored living with the Husband Judge. Mavis is also worried she will be a prime suspect in the recent murder—last night—of The Cad Judge." Frank told it like he was delivering a dossier.

"How did you figure all this out?" I whispered.

"Oh, Mavis and I had a glass of wine for lunch, no food, just wine. She spilled it all, the facts not the wine. What else do you want to know?"

"Just her daughter and a male friend of hers. She introduced him as the widow somebody or other. A friend of her and her ex, but it looks like he's more her friend now," he said.

"You never cease to amaze me, Frank."

"I'm not just a pretty face in a concierge or maid uniform," he whispered.

"You are the master and I am the grasshopper," I said. Frank was a source of constant entertainment and information. Then he told me to wait until he left, count to one hundred before I left the hall closet. He opened the door a crack, peeked out, looked both ways and slipped out into the great expanse of the guest house hallway reception area.

I really hoped Frank and I would play spy again soon. He didn't tell me anything I didn't already know, but it was amazing he uncovered that much in such a short time.

When I stepped out into the hall Frank was standing at the reception desk. When he saw me he said loudly so the entire mansion could hear him, "Miss Brandy Alexander, why it's been a while since you graced us with your delightful self."

"Frank!" Julia screamed from somewhere upstairs. "Is Brandy here? Send her up."

JULIA WAS SITTING in her office upstairs which was one end of a double parlor with the other end as her bedroom, or as Frank described it, Julia's playpen. Frank also said it was very convenient for her to have salesmen or clients meet in her office at one end of the room with a bed at the other. She dressed like she stepped out of a VOGUE magazine. Today she was wearing a pink, Chanel suit with black fringe. She looked stunning. Being tall, thin with lots of auburn hair didn't hurt either, however she was still into the Dallas Big Hair thing. She needed a new do, but neither Frank nor I would be the ones to tell her.

Woozie, who was the housekeeper in my family since I came home from the hospital, had sent her sister, Gloria to work for Julia. I tried to dissuade that arrangement knowing how brutal it could be working for a demanding perfectionist like Julia. Just ask Frank.

Woozie helped at Julia's bed and breakfast right after she opened and they found a dead body in one of the rooms the next morning. Julia needed some TLC during that timeframe. Frank and Woozie filled in for me when I was working or couldn't be there. That lasted about a month until my dad demanded Woozie return to my parents' home to cook, not clean so much, for them. Then Woozie referred Gloria to the guest house in her place.

Gloria was standing next to Julia holding a silver tray with a glass of water and a glass of wine on it. I struggled not to laugh out loud imaging Frank in the wig and uniform. Gloria was going about putting Julia's wine and water, one by one, onto coasters on Julia's desk. She was wearing a black dress with a white apron and a white hat. I had seen a similar hat bobby-pinned to the hidden wig Frank showed me downstairs. Julia was putting stamps on envelopes and putting the envelopes on Gloria's tray in place of the wine and water.

"Brandy, you wanna glass of wine?" Julia asked when I stepped into the room. As I sat in the chair opposite her she looked up at me and asked, "What's so funny? Why are you smiling like that?"

"Just happy to see you," I said. "Gloria, water is fine for me," I said.

Julia keep her eyes on me as if trying to figure out if I was lying, and slowly turned to look at Gloria at this point. "Gloria, please bring Brandy a Pellegrino…" she said looking up at Gloria for the first time. Her head jerked back, and she asked, "Gloria, where is your wig? I hope you haven't left it on the hall tree again downstairs, or on the coffee table in the waiting room."

"No, Miz Julia. I puts it in my purse so it not be out on any table so a guest can sees it."

"I didn't see it anywhere on my way up here," I said trying to give Gloria some backup. "Please, Gloria, ice water from the tap is fine."

"Tap water? Don't you listen to the news? That can kill you. They only recently lifted the boil water advisory again, but I'm not drinking anything that's not bottled and neither should you," Julia said. "Gloria, bring her a bottled water. Cold."

I gave Gloria my 'what can you do but agree with her smile' while Julia went on with her rant.

"It's like we live in a third world country in New Orleans. Boil water, humph. Can you see New York, LA or Chicago sending out boil water advisories to residents? They'd be up in arms if their sewerage and water boards couldn't keep water clean enough to drink. Why should everyone have to boil it before you drink or shower? They even warn against showering with water straight out of the tap if you have any open wounds or cuts. This must be popular with the hotels in the French Quarter with all those drunken tourists all hot and sweaty from drinking all day on Bourbon Street. Besides how do you boil water in a hotel room?"

"That's a good question." It was always better to agree with Julia when it didn't matter. "I showered already before I heard the advisory. Oh, well," I said. "I came here to ask you something about one of your guests."

"Oh, no, not the ex-wife of that murdered judge?"

"That's the one," I said. "You are telepathic. You could open a table downstairs and charge to read people's minds. That could be another income stream for you."

Julia stopped what she was doing, which was a lot of nothing, and put her hands together on her desk. She looked at me and smiled. Her curiosity was piqued. "What cha wanna know?" she asked tying her best to sound helpful.

"I remember you telling me you were going to install a security system with cameras. Did you ever do that?" I asked.

"Yes," she answered and her eyes narrowed. "Right now, there are only cameras on the front door and back door. I'm thinking of adding two more, one on each side of the building. Why?"

That would be bad for Frank's secret escape route.

"Do you have or do you save the footage? I'm only interested in what you have from last night." I asked. "I need to find out if Mavis Martin, your guest, left here at any time on Friday and what time she got back."

"Frank could tell you without the camera footage. He's better than the security system, but don't tell him I said that," she said. "Does this have to do with her being a suspect? That murdered judge was all over the news this morning."

"I'd like the camera footage if only to clear her. Jiff is representing her ex-husband," I said. "He's worried the police will arrest her. I went to college with Bas and Mavis."

"Let her attorney do that if she's arrested," Julia said. Julia wasn't big on showing kindness to strangers, or friends either, for that matter.

"Well, her husband, also a judge, doesn't want their only daughter to have to visit their mother in Saint Gabriel's Prison for Women," I said. "That's my take on it."

"Frank said she was drinking yesterday, all afternoon. She told him how she was involved with Judge Whitmer and how it destroyed her marriage. Then the no-good—I'm not sure what to call him—dumped her for a younger model," Julia said. "It figures her ex-husband wants to keep her out of jail. Who will help him with their kid? How will he have free time to find another wife if he has to watch the kid?"

"Julia, c'mon. Would you want to see your mother arrested for murder and possibly go to jail?" I asked.

"Not my mother, but my dad was another story. I would have testified myself if it put him in jail. My mother, my brother and I had a horrible life with him," she said. "I only wish my mother would have outlived him so she would have found some peace for a while."

Julia didn't talk much about her family, and I recently found out her dad abused them. Julia had come into some money when her dad died then her brother was murdered. She didn't need to work or keep the guest house open, but she liked the independence that came with owning your own business. For the most part, it suited her.

"Please, Julia?" I asked.

"Fine. I'll get Frank to burn you a CD with the last 48 hours on it. Will that do it?" She picked up her phone and texted. I assumed she was sending instructions to Frank. Julia was efficient.

"I believe it will," I said. "And thanks, on behalf of Jiff. He will appreciate it."

"It's the least I can do for him. He's saved my…he saved me in the past," she said. "Frank will have it for you when you are ready to leave. I texted him to do it."

"There's something else I want to ask you," I said.

"Only one favor per day," she said taking a sip of wine. "Just kidding, ask away."

"What do you know about an app called Find-Me.com for dogs? I think it's a GPS tracking system that works like a microchip in a dog's collar. Have you heard of it?"

Julia didn't like people much, but she loved dogs. She had five or seven, I could never remember exactly. We had the love of dogs in common.

"Yeah, I've heard about it and thought about getting it for my dogs. I haven't completely researched it," she said.

Darn. When Julia researched it, there was no need for me to. If it got the Julia white glove seal of approval, no alternative was worth spending my time on to consider.

"Go online and Google it," she said. That was Julia's response to all questions she didn't have an answer for, which usually wasn't many. She was right. I would go to the source and that was their website.

"Hey, I'd still like to speak to Mavis Martin. Is she around?"

"Go ask Frank. He's probably chilling the wine for the two of them as we speak," she said.

"That's a good idea," I said standing up. "I only have one question for her. The security footage ought to attest to her whereabouts. I have a dinner date with Jiff a little later. I need to pick up Meaux from the groomer and get home in time to freshen up."

"You better not keep that man waiting or I'll steal him from you. He's a prince of a guy, and you know I don't say that too often."

"Right. I'll let you know what I find out about the GPS for the dogs," I said. I didn't want to tell her it might have something to do with the judge's murderer.

🐐 🐐 🐐 🐐 🐐 🐐 🐐 🐐 🐐 🐐

DOWNSTAIRS ON THE veranda, Frank was pouring two

glasses of Chardonnay for Mavis and himself.

"Miss Alexander, will you be joining us?" Frank asked as soon as I walked up.

"No, well…maybe. That looks good," I said smiling at Mavis who appeared to be well past her first glass of wine.

"Take my glass and sit here with Miss Mavis Martin. Miss Martin this is a good friend of the owner's and mine, Miss Brandy Alexander." Frank started the introduction, but I interrupted him.

"We are acquainted with each other. I've been to the Martin home as a guest in the past. Thank you, Frank."

He put the second glass in front of me saying, "I'll go get myself another glass." Frank was a lot more intuitive than Julia.

"Mavis, I'm sorry to hear about Whit. To his memory," I said lifting my glass to hers.

"That's a good idea. We have had lots of good memories over the years," she was speaking deliberately. "It's only recently that things took a turn."

"Yes, I have great memories of him also," I said, not wanting to get into what provoked the turn. "To Whit."

"To Whit," she said.

We clinked our wine glasses, and each took a sip.

"I'm sure his golfing buddies will miss him. Whit loved golf," I said not knowing how else to bring up the gambling. Mavis might not be aware of the debts, who he owed or how he paid them.

"Some," she said and took a big sip of wine, "more than others."

She wasn't slurring her words yet, but she was on her way.

"Jiff played with Whit and Bas from time to time," I said trying to keep her talking about the golfing friends. "Jiff lost a few bucks in one game to the others and he's not a big gambler."

"Whit was an additional income stream for two of his golfing pals," Mavis continued. "Pierre often joked the money Whit lost to him paid for his kids' college funds."

"Who did he play with?" I asked. "I know Jiff said he played with Whit from time to time."

"Jiff didn't play but once or twice as a stand in for Bas. Whit and Bas used to play with August Randolph and Pierre LeBlanc. Bas said 'Whit often lost to August or Pierre or both.' Bas always let Whit slide from paying what he owed him," Mavis said deliberately, enunciating every word. "I told Bas he should let Whit pay him. It might have slowed down his gambling."

Frank came back with the third glass of wine ready to join us.

"Wow, I've lost track of the time, Frank. I must run. I hope to see you again soon, Mavis," I said and saw Frank slide the CD into my purse when Mavis wasn't looking.

Chapter Eleven

JUSTICE AND MEAUX chased each other through my house at full speed. I opened the back door so the yard could be part of the track. One would chase the other at full speed until the chasing schnauzer body-slammed the other. In the blink of an eye they froze in place. Then they switched who was being chased by the other and off they went again.

I missed having two dogs in my home. I was between rescues until Justice. Meaux loved to play and I called him the Doggie Ambassador. He could get all dogs to play and be a dog again, no matter how scared or mistreated they had been before they came to us.

There wasn't much time to sit and watch them play so after a few minutes, I jumped in the shower. I changed into a little black dress that dipped low in the back. I fluffed out my shoulder length hair I had had in a ponytail all day. Once I felt ready to meet Jiff for our evening, I pulled out the disk Frank burned and slipped it into my computer. In the sleeve I found a note from Frank that said, *Here is the login and password should you want to see anything else. It deletes files after a week.*

Don't tell the Queen or I shall be drawn and quartered before the pig is roasted and served at the grand banquet.

I guess Frank stopped playing secret agent and was now Medieval Frank.

After I watched about five minutes of mind-numbing video with Julia, Frank, Mavis and Gloria going in and out of the front door, I hit fast forward. It's easier to see when someone did anything out of the ordinary with the video speeded up because the rhythm of the video changed. There was Frank, taking something out of the desk and putting it in his pocket after looking around to see if Julia caught him. Gloria came in, removed her wig and looked for a place to store it. She finally decided to put it in her purse.

Mavis came in and out only once during the entire time in question, but she stood inside at the entry door as if she was waiting for someone at 7:55 p.m. She stayed inside peeking out through the leaded glass. She wrapped her long hair around her finger all the way to her head, released it and wrapped it in the opposite direction. She opened the door and Marigny walked in wearing a black baseball cap. The video timestamp showed 8:00 p.m. Seeing them together made me think how much they looked and dressed alike.

Once inside the two hugged. There seemed to be a brief exchange before Marigny wiped her eyes. She appeared to be crying. They put their arms around each other's waist as they walked into the dark parlor off the main hallway entrance. They didn't stay long, and they didn't turn on a light that could be seen from the hall camera.

About four and a half minutes later, Mavis walked Marigny back to the front door. She held a card or piece of paper in her hand. Mavis put the paper in one of her pockets and when she opened the door, Bas was standing there. It seemed they had a heated exchange before Bas grabbed Marigny's hand and pulled her along with him. They left in a hurry.

The doorbell rang sending Meaux and Justice into a barking frenzy. It was Jiff coming to pick me up for our dinner date. Swinging the front door open wide, I blurted out, "Wait until you see Julia's security footage."

Jiff stood there holding a bouquet of roses allowing my announcement to register. He extended his hand with the flowers, he always brought me roses, pink this time. "Can it wait until after dinner?"

"Well…maybe. The important part isn't long. I'll queue it up. We can watch it, go to dinner so we can talk about it, then come back here and see it again if you like."

"Something tells me this security tape will take over our evening," Jiff said following me to the computer still holding the flowers.

"Take a quick look then we can decide what to do." I sat at my computer and rewound the footage to where Mavis waited at the front door.

Who was I kidding? A quick look?

After we watched the footage, I speeded up the four and a half minutes of Mavis and Marigny in the parlor. Jiff asked me to play it again while he took notes on the times.

"I think we should give this to the police, if they haven't gone looking for it already," I said. "I'll call Frank and see if the police asked for it yet."

"I'm sure they have and they're watching it as we speak." Jiff slumped down in one of my dining room chairs. "You know what this means?"

"Your job just got a lot harder since the judge, and his daughter were not where they told you or the police they were last night. And, this tape catches them in a lie."

"You have no idea."

"Look on the bright side, Mavis is cleared," I said.

Jiff looked at me and rolled his eyes.

"You should have seen her, Jiff. This afternoon she was plastered at 4:30 p.m. and Frank was bringing her another glass of wine. She wasn't slurring her words yet, but was well on her way."

"I promised to take you to dinner. Let's go eat then we'll come back and decide what to do. A break from this is what I need. Let's have the nice evening I planned while these new fun facts process in my head. It might be the last one for a while if Bas or Marigny get arrested."

"I'll make a quick call to Frank to see if the police have this yet. Then, we'll know how much wine we can have for dinner," I said as I put my arms around his waist. I watched a smile sneak out of the corners of his mouth while I started to feel all warm inside.

Chapter Twelve

WHILE JIFF DROVE, I called Julia's guest house to speak to Frank. It was a few minutes after 7:00 p.m. on a Saturday evening. Julia answered, "Canal Street Bed and Breakfast."

"Julia, why are you answering your phones? Where's Frank?"

"I'm sorry but our concierge is busy right now. Can I take a message or can someone else help you?"

I held my cell away from my ear and looked at it. Why was Julia talking like this? Had the body snatchers invaded Julia's bed and breakfast and this was her replacement? Was I talking to one of them instead of Julia who was now somewhere asleep, forever in a pod?

"Julia, it's me, Brandy. Didn't you recognize my number, or my voice?"

"Yes, of course. I'm happy to take a message for Frank and have him return your call once he finishes making a copy of our security footage to send with the police."

"The police are there?"

"Yes, he's busy right now, but if you want to call

back, he should be free in an hour." Julia paused and then added as if she was answering questions I was asking, "That's fine. Yes. Thank you, I'll tell him. Goodbye."

I turned to Jiff driving. "According to Julia—who is answering the guest house phones and is a lot more covert than I ever gave her credit for—we have an hour or so before Frank finishes copying the security footage for the police. It seems they are standing there waiting for it."

"Great. That means a short dinner or even take out," he said rubbing his forehead between his eyes in a circular motion.

"Maybe not. Why don't we go to Santa Fe?" I said putting my hand on his arm nearest me. "It's close, easy parking, and it's nice this evening. We can sit outside— have a glass of wine—relax, and if we need to get dinner to go, then we'll be all set."

"That's a good idea," he answered. "Sitting outside on Esplanade for an hour or so will be just what I need before I have to jump back into this mess."

"If Frank is dilly dallying around copying that footage, that means the police won't get back to the precinct to view it for at least an hour. Frank is probably copying everything that's recorded and not just the last twenty-four hours for them. It will take them awhile to watch it all. We can at least order and enjoy dinner," I said. "I don't think we need to swallow it in one bite."

"As soon as they discover what we discovered, they're going to beeline it to Bas' home to question him and Marigny. Or they'll call me to bring them in for questioning."

"Do you think you need to call and warn him?" I asked.

"I'd have to say, oh gee, Bas, I just saw a security tape of you that proves you lied to me and the police last night. And oh, yeah, by the way, the police are getting a copy of it now. Whatcha wanna do about that, pal?" he said thumping the steering wheel on every syllable. "They will probably ask that he turn himself in at a particular time if they decide to charge him. There's also the matter of Marigny lying. It begs the bigger questions—why did they? What are they hiding, and how much does Mavis know?"

Jiff parked, came over to my side to open my door and we walked to the hostess stand. We requested an outside table and were seated near the fountain. A waiter left menus with us after taking our drink orders. When he left to fetch our drinks I said, "Let's pinky swear we will not talk about this until the check comes." I held up my right hand in a fist with the little finger out like a hook.

"I feel like I'm five years old," Jiff said quick to wrap his pinky in mine. We held it there a second, smiled at each other and then we pulled apart.

"That's when pinky swearing was common and held more power and commitment than a handshake does today. Remember?" I said.

"I do remember, and you're right."

Two glasses of wine came, and we toasted to a lovely evening, sitting outside under the veranda looking over the menus. My friend, Lollie, who owns the restaurant came out and gave me a kiss on each cheek. I introduced Jiff who had not met her. She suggested the special of the day just before someone called her back into the kitchen.

The humidity was low, so it made for a delightful evening outdoors. Our clothes were not sticking to us due to perspiring while sitting still. The drop was an NOLA weather sign that fall was on its way—low humidity and a thermostat that registered just under one hundred degrees. There was an intermittent breeze that actually felt quite nice. We ordered Gazpacho soup as an appetizer and Lollie's recommendations. Jiff ordered the ceviche special of the day which was loaded with shrimp, fish, calamari and avocado. I had a salad with jumbo crab meat. We both needed a go box for our leftovers.

As soon as Jiff paid for dinner, his cellphone rang. It was Bas.

"Hey, Bas. Can I call you right back? I'm just leaving a restaurant and I'll be in my car in a few minutes," he said, waited for a response, then hung up.

Inside Jiff's Mercedes, which felt like we were inside a vacuum when the doors closed, I asked, "Is this your version of the Cone of Silence? Frank has one too. It's the hall closet under the stairs at Julia's guest house. I was in it yesterday."

Jiff didn't answer. He usually laughs at my jokes, but he didn't smile, he sat there thinking, his back ramrod straight looking at nothing in particular ahead of him. He had not started the car. He pulled out his cellphone. Before he rang Bas back he said, "I'm sorry. You had nothing to do with this except find out the truth, and you gave me a heads up. Bas knows how hard this is going to be now. If he had just told the truth, we could have worked with it. Now, I want to strangle him and his daughter. I won't be able to represent them both, and Marigny will probably need an attorney. She makes it much more difficult to defend her father."

"The more I think about what I saw on that tape is a little confusing," I said. "Why did Marigny go to Mavis? She must have called her dad and told him she was going there since he showed up shortly after she did. How did he know Marigny had gone to see her mother unless Marigny or Mavis called him? Why did he lie? He said Marigny had been home since 4:00 p.m. that afternoon with him?"

"Good questions. Did Marigny go see Whit? It seems like it now, and if she did, what is her Dad hoping to cover or shield her from?" Jiff mused out loud.

"We're forgetting an important part of all this," I said.

"Right, the money. Who took the money? And if Marigny went to see Whit why would she take it?" Jiff asked out loud.

"She wouldn't. Her parents give her whatever she wants. She told me she was getting her dad's Mercedes when she passes her driver's test next week. I don't think money had anything to do with why she went to see him, then ran crying to her mother. I think it's something else," I said.

"You're right, but what was it? And what time was she there? Was Whit alive? Maybe she found him dead?" Jiff took notes on a small leather pad he kept in his inside suit pocket with his Mont Blanc pen.

Hmm. Jiff and Taylor seemed to have more in common than wearing well coordinated suits.

"Why don't I drive us back to my house while you take notes and decide what you want to ask him when you call Bas back" I said.

"Great idea," he said. We both changed seats, and I was about to drive us back to my place when Jiff changed his mind.

"Please drive straight to Bas' house. I want to look him and Marigny in the eye when I ask them these questions," Jiff said scribbling away in his notepad.

I PULLED UP in front of the Bas Martin's home and parked in the street. The driveway had two police cars already parked there. One was the car Hanky drove with her partner, Detective Travis and the other was

Dante's police vehicle.

"Great. This is gonna be just great," Jiff moaned. "Nothing like making something harder than it has to be."

"How did they see that tape so fast?" I wondered out loud.

"All their cars have computers now, making the police almost as fast as the criminals," Jiff said as his cellphone rang. "It's Bas again." He answered his call. "Bas, I'm out front, and coming in now. Don't say anything to the police."

Chapter Thirteen

JUDGE BAS MARTIN, Marigny Martin, Captain Dante Deedler, Detectives Hanky and Taylor were all standing in a circle, in the living room of the Martin home. No one was speaking when Jiff and I were ushered into by the manservant. It looked like a Mexican standoff.

Dante did an ever so slight double take when he saw me with Jiff and Detective Taylor smiled. Hanky just did a long blink so as not to roll her eyes. Yep, I imagined they were thinking *here she is again.* I nodded to them.

Jiff nodded to Dante, Hanky and Taylor adding by way of a greeting, "Captain. Detectives."

Dante started in. "We believe Judge Martin and his daughter Marigny are involved in the murder of Judge Whitmer. We'd like to take them in for questioning."

"Are they being arrested?" Jiff asked. When no one answered, he added, "I represent them, so if you have questions, we're happy to answer them. First, I'd like a moment alone with them, if you don't mind," Jiff said. He held his arm out indicating they should go wait in the hall.

Dante, Travis and Hanky left the room.

Jiff asked, "Bas, tell me now why you and Marigny were not home the night Whit was killed. Did they tell you they have you on the security tape at the bed and breakfast where Mavis is staying?"

Marigny and Bas looked at each other. Marigny started sobbing and Bas said, "It's not what you think."

"Then tell me what it is," Jiff said. "Brandy, do you mind waiting out there with the police? Please keep an eye on them so they're not eavesdropping."

🐾 🐾 🐾 🐾 🐾 🐾 🐾 🐾 🐾 🐾

"WELL, NOW IT'S a party," Detective Taylor said smiling when I stepped into the hall closing the double parlor doors behind me.

Hanky and Dante had their police faces on.

"Has anyone seen Mr. Walters?" I asked.

"Mr. Walters?" Taylor asked. "Who's that?"

"The Martins' manservant or butler. I'm not sure what his official title is," I said. "He must be off tonight. I know my way to the kitchen," I said turning and heading that way. Over my shoulder I asked, "Does anyone want a glass of water, coke or a cup of coffee?"

Reluctantly, the three followed me.

In the kitchen I opened cabinets and found coffee, sugar and creamers putting them out on the counter.

"No doughnuts?" Detective Taylor asked.

"I had you pegged for a cruller man," I said.

"A what?" he asked.

"Oh, a cruller is a special French type doughnut. I guess it hasn't migrated above the Mason Dixon line into Brooklyn. Isn't that where you're from?" I asked him.

"It's a twisted oblong pastry. It tastes like a doughnut only looks like a spiral with a ridged surface, topped with icing," Hanky said.

"You know your doughnuts," I said. "I guess you can't help but know how many different kinds there are. It seems everyone in the department spends a lot of time eating doughnuts. You can't drive past a doughnut shop in this city and not see police cars parked out front."

"The doughnut jokes are getting old," Dante said. He was not amused and the vein on the side of his head bulged. I could see every heart beat play out in it. I had teased him enough over the years about taking breaks in doughnut shops, but wondered if it wasn't me teasing Taylor that had the vein working overtime.

"Give it a little time, Detective Taylor, and you, too, will be a doughnut connoisseur," I said making a pot of coffee. Dante and I always seemed to find ourselves discussing...or rather...disagreeing...over coffee.

We sat drinking a cup of coffee around the enormous, white marble-topped kitchen island.

"My whole apartment in New York was just about

the size of this marble slab," Detective Taylor said. "Not the size of this entire kitchen. Just the marble on top this island."

"Then you must have had to step outside to change your mind," I said. "Does that mean you don't get to think much in New York unless you're outside?"

Taylor smiled at me shaking his head.

Dante was deep in thought studying the steam coming out of his coffee cup. I tapped him on the arm and said, "If I tell you something I learned late this afternoon will you consider what I have to say?"

All three sat up a little straighter. Taylor and Hanky drank their coffee. Dante was not going to like this.

"What is it?" Dante asked.

"I'm not going to ask you for information. I have some for you," I said.

Hanky and Taylor leaned toward me.

Dante looked back and forth at each of the detectives and exhaled heavily before saying, "Go on."

"I got a call from the shelter across the river this afternoon," I said.

"Across the river?" Taylor asked.

"The Mississippi River, the West Bank Animal Shelter," Hanky answered Taylor but kept her eyes on me.

"The shelter manager called me because they found a dog tied to the fence this morning. It was Whit's dog, Justice."

"How are you so sure it's his dog?" Dante asked

with a little to much edge in his voice for my taste.

Oh, brother, this was going to be a fun discussion.

"Because it has a microchip and each microchip number is associated to an owner or a rescue, in my case, it gets registered to me," I said.

"All those dogs look alike, maybe they got the microchip numbers mixed up," Taylor said.

"No, I'm positive it's his dog," I said.

"How are you so sure it's the judge's dog?" Dante asked.

"I'm sure. Besides the microchip number and the fact that I recognize differences in each dog, this dog had Neuticles," I said.

"It had what?" Dante asked finally looking up from his coffee.

"Neuticles. I didn't have them put in the dog," I said. "The person who adopted him from me did. It's not common and in this case, I can vouch it was Judge Whitmer. I don't change the microchip out of my name because I want to keep track of any rescues that are escaping from yards and how often. That's why the shelter called me to claim him."

"What are Neuticals?" Taylor asked with the same questioning look on his face when I first mentioned them.

I looked at Hanky hoping she could put it in cop speak for Dante and explain it to him but she shrugged not knowing what they were either.

"Neuticals are implants to create fake testicles. After

a neuter, a dog's testicles shrink, sometimes completely disappearing. Some men, like Whit, want their dogs to appear more…more…male, I guess. I really can't imagine anyone being so insecure that they need their dog to have visible testicles," I said.

Dante and Taylor wore expressions that suggested they found the whole idea painful as if they were getting Neuticles implanted after being neutered themselves.

Hanky just rolled her eyes.

"So, what do you suggest we can do with that info?" Dante asked.

"Actually, the dog is registered and belongs to me. He was found tied to the shelter fence, sitting in a pothole filled with water. He was a muddy, wet mess. The shelter hosed him off and let him dry by the time I got there."

"We should have our techs look at him," Dante said.

"No. You will keep him in some quarantine for months until this case resolves and by that time he will be depressed and possibly dead. Most likely whoever took the dog to the shelter murdered Whit," I said.

"Do you want us to ask the dog who gave him a ride to the shelter?" Dante said.

I wanted to slap him and from the look on Hanky's face; she did too. Taylor sat stone-faced.

"There might be a way he can tell us. Get your tech guys to see if there is a program on Whit's computer, like a GPS, that tracks his dog," I said.

Dante just looked at me. I could tell he didn't buy into any of it and the vein on the side of his head began to pulsate.

"If you find a GPS...thing...on that dog, you call me asap, or, or, or..." he trailed off.

"You'll arrest me for withholding evidence," I finished for him. "Look, I'm aware you have that security tape from the bed and breakfast."

"Who told you that?" Dante demanded.

"Why? Was it a secret? You should be glad people don't keep secrets about this kinda stuff. If everyone kept secrets, how would you ever solve anything?" I asked. Okay, that comment got the vein on the side of his forehead to bulge even more.

"How do you know the daughter didn't take the dog to the West Bank Animal Shelter after she killed the judge and before she visited the mom?" Dante asked. "Maybe her Judge Daddy killed his buddy for stepping out with his wife. Either way, they are lying to us."

"Perhaps they are lying but I don't think it's because one of them killed Whit. Maybe it's something else." I said.

Taylor and Hanky were looking around the kitchen acting as if they didn't hear Dante and I arguing right in front of them. They drifted over to the microwave to examine it more closely, like shoppers in an appliance store.

"Why do you feel a need to put your foot in my cases? Can't you just leave it alone and let the police do what we're paid to do?" he snapped at me.

"I'm not trying to do your job...." I told him but was cut off when Jiff appeared at the kitchen entrance.

Jiff looked at me and Dante, then at Hanky and Taylor inspecting the microwave. "I've advised them not to answer any question. Unless you are going to arrest someone, I think we're done for the night."

Dante looked like he would explode. His skin was beginning to color a brilliant red hue on his neck and was working up his face—he was truly ticked off.

"If we have to, we'll come back with a warrant," Dante said.

"If you get a warrant, please call my office and I'll bring them in for questioning. Good evening," Jiff said by way of telling them it was time to leave.

🐐 🐐 🐐 🐐 🐐 🐐 🐐 🐐 🐐 🐐

AFTER THE POLICE left, we said good night to Bas and Marigny.

"We'll probably have to answer questions after they get a warrant," Jiff said to Bas. "You should consider getting Marigny an attorney to represent her in case they push this and want to arrest the two of you, and we don't find the real killer soon."

In the car Jiff said, "They didn't have anything to do with the dog at the shelter or the murder. They have a great big motive for either or both of them killing

Whit. The police could arrest them over it in a heartbeat."

"Like what?" I asked. "The police know Bas and Marigny lied to them."

"Yes, they lied to the police. But, the police don't know why. Whit was threatening Marigny to post nude photos he took of Mavis on the internet. He took them or Mavis sent them to him while they were having their affair. Whit threatened Marigny to post her mother's photos if she didn't pose for one in exchange."

"Wait. What? I knew Whit had girly photos...well...porn, actually. He kept it in his bedside table." I said and hurriedly added when Jiff's head jerked in my direction, "Claudette told me that. She said he would cut photos out of magazines and keep them in his wallet. I guess he got tired of not knowing them personally."

"How could Mavis be so...so...naïve?" Jiff asked as if pondering the idea.

"I was going to say, stupid. How could Mavis be so stupid? She doesn't strike me as a dummy," I said. "A drinker, yes, but a dimwit, no."

"Marigny said Whit called her and asked her to come over to show her something. I guess he was drunk, and Justine left so he was looking to spice up his Monday night," Jiff said.

"He should have turned on Monday Night Football," I said.

"The season hasn't started yet," Jiff said looking

flummoxed. "The Super Bowl was two months ago, remember?"

"I watched the Puppy Bowl," I said. "Are they even at the same time?"

"You like the commercials, I know you do," he said.

"What? Never mind football. What time was she at Whit's? Do you remember seeing Marigny hand Mavis something she put in her pocket on the tape? That could have been one of Whit's nude photos of Mavis. If Marigny got that photo, does that mean she let Whit take a photo of her? If the police check Whit's computer they will probably find more," I said.

"Yes, and that's not all. Marigny said she walked from home to Whit's house. She had been home studying since four o'clock like Bas told the police. Her Dad wasn't aware she left until Mavis called him and said she was on her way to the guest house. Mavis told Bas the whole story about the nude photos. That gives him a motive for killing Whit. After Whit tried to get Marigny to pose nude for him in exchange for her Mom's photos, she ran out pushing the front door open and leaving it like that," Jiff said.

"So, her fingerprints are all over the inside of the door."

"Maybe, along with everyone else who goes in and out. She says she ran up to St. Charles Avenue and called an Uber to pick her up and take her to her Mom. She called Mavis on the way there," he said.

"That explains why Mavis was waiting for her. I bet Whit gave her a photo to blackmail that young girl into posing nude," I said.

"Probably, but now it looks like Mavis or Bas killed Whit over it," Jiff said.

"The Uber taxi record and the security tapes prove the time Bas and Marigny were at the guest house, but it won't clear them. The time of death is too close to their time there," I said. "Did she see anyone waiting or pull up when she left?"

"She didn't say, or rather says she didn't notice. She wanted out of there," Jiff said.

"Well, ask her because if she didn't drive over to Whit's, then who was in the black Mercedes? Mr. Mouton saw someone drive up when he picked up their dinner," I said.

We both said at the same time, "Whoever stole the money and killed Whit."

"Right, so we need to concentrate on Whit's gambling debts. We need to talk to Justine," Jiff said.

"I told Dante, Hanky and Taylor where I found Whit's dog. Dante didn't seem to care," I said.

"I'm glad you did, though. Hopefully, Hanky or Taylor will look into it. They don't seem to have the need to be the Knight in Shining Armor in front of you like Dante does," Jiff said.

I could only imagine how Jiff would react if he knew Dante ran background checks on him and his family!

Chapter Fourteen

BACK AT MY house we watched the security tape again. Jiff included me in everything. He always valued my opinion and what I had to say. Jiff often said I had a knack for finding the smallest detail or fact everyone else missed or overlooked.

"The timestamp on the tape could also be Bas and Marigny's alibi," I said. "Look at both. If one of them shot Whit fifteen times, wouldn't they have blood on their clothes? At least whoever picked up Justice and drove him to the shelter should have had blood on them or in their car."

"They should. They both look distraught enough on this tape for something to have happened, but murder? How could Marigny, all ninety pounds of her, get the best of Whit, tie him up then shoot him?"

"He was drunk. Maybe she said the only way she'd take off her clothes for him was if she tied him up. I think Whit would go for that. From the open decanter on his desk and the half glass of whiskey, it looks like he drank more after he got home last night," I said.

"Would Marigny think fast enough to make an

offer like that to Whit? Telling him to let her tie him up? You know, it kinda scares me when you come up with things like that," he said watching me carefully.

"I don't believe Marigny thought like that, because she was acting like a girl who needed to talk to her mother, not a girl who just killed someone," I said.

"Whoever killed him was very careful not to leave bloody footprints. You're right. They had to be close enough to shoot him. They would have gotten gunshot residue on them or their clothes and most likely blood splatter, at least in their car. At the very least, they should have gotten some in their car if they took Justice."

Jiff was wound up and pacing. I poured us each a glass of wine and placed his next to his chair.

"Let's watch this once more," I said. "C'mon, sit down and have a glass of wine with me. We can see it again tomorrow morning," I said. I ushered him to the chair in front of the computer. I stood behind him and rubbed his shoulders to help him relax.

"Tomorrow morning, we need to remember everything we can from the time we got to Lancey's, left, and I got to Whit's home. The timeline on Whit's murder will narrow down who could have killed him. I think it's someone who knew exactly where he was that night," I said and leaned over to whisper in his ear. "Your neck is so tense, and I know something that will help you relax."

"I think it will help you relax too," he said and

pulled me into his lap to kiss me.

🐐 🐐 🐐 🐐 🐐 🐐 🐐 🐐 🐐 🐐

TWO WET DOG noses greeted us on Sunday morning. Justice and Meaux were better than an alarm clock and they let me know they wanted to go outside by 7:00 a.m.

"Isn't this a little early for you two?" Jiff asked smiling and rubbing their heads as they pounced on him when they realized we were awake. "I'm glad I left Isabella at my parents' home yesterday."

"Usually, Meaux wakes me up at 6:00 a.m. He's got company so I guess he decided to sleep in," I said getting up to go let them out into my backyard.

"Come back so we can relax a little more before we start our day," he said. The thought of that man kissing me made me all but jump back into bed with him.

Later, after I fed the dogs and made a pot of New Orleans coffee with chicory, the only coffee allowed in my kitchen, we recounted how the evening at Lancey's unfolded. Jiff and I worked well together. He treated me like a consultant on his cases. I loved it. I sat in when his investigators worked with the clients at a conference table and recounted every detail that could be recalled from the event. No detail was overlooked. Everything was entered into a timeline, no matter how small. The problem with this one was Bas claimed he never went to Whit's house that night, but Marigny did. We had her timeline based on the Uber receipt and the security footage from Julia's bed and breakfast.

"Let's work with all the times we are sure of on a timeline to see where the holes are," I said.

Jiff started. "We got to Lancey's at different times but left together at 7: 30 p.m."

"I wasn't there long before Justine moved Whit along to leave, and that was about 6:30 p.m." I said. "Justine left with Whit but two of his friends walked out at the same time. Did you see them shake Whit's hand? They seemed very serious. I didn't think much of it at the time."

"I was probably looking at you, so no, I didn't see them. Do you remember who they were?" Jiff asked.

"I didn't remember their names but I knew them from the Krewe of Orpheus. Mavis told me their names when I spoke with her. I rode on Whit's float one year and those two were riders as well. That night at Lancey's they stood off from the more celebratory group and only spoke to each other. When Whit left back slapping his pals, they both stepped in front of him to block his way out. So Whit, with his tall, lanky self, sort of pushed between them to leave. It didn't look unfriendly, but it wasn't friendly either," I said.

"They were standing at the far end of the bar closest to the door. They had on dark suits. When I walked in, I passed them and saw they were both tall and nice looking. One had a very full head of dark hair, was a bit taller, like five-eleven or six feet, and more fit. I noticed a GMP-Master Rolex on his hand holding his drink.

He was drinking something clear, vodka or gin while the other guy had less hair—okay—he was balding, had a honey-colored bourbon or whiskey drink in an old fashion glass."

"Wow, you might turn into an investigator yet. That sounds like August Randolph and Pierre Le-Blanc—Whit's golf buddies. Whit teased August calling him the Bald Cajun and said Pierre was the Handsome Frenchman," Jiff said. "It raked on August's nerves."

"Whit had a way of needling someone once he determined something irked them. Then, he harped on it in front of everyone," I said.

"Yep."

"Those are the names Mavis gave me as Whit's golfing buddies. They left more or less at the same time as Whit and Justine. One of them could have followed him home. Mr. Mouton said he left at 7:00 p.m. to pick up his dinner order and was back by 7:30 p.m. He saw a car drive up, a black sedan," I said. I looked at what Jiff wrote. "Whoever drove that car knows something we don't or is the murderer."

We documented the following as we remembered it:

6:30 p.m. Whit and Justine leave Lancey's w/golf buddies following

6:45 p.m. Justine drops off Whit (Does not go in per Mr. Mouton)

6:50 p.m. Marigny goes to Whit's house, Uber receipt is for a 7:30 p.m. pick up on St. Charles Ave. She needs a few minutes to walk/run to St. Charles and wait on Uber. Puts her at Whit's about 6:50 p.m., out by 7:05 p.m. When she leaves, she says he is alive.

7:05-7:40 p.m. someone kills Whit (Person in black or dark sedan Mr. Mouton sees) and takes money

7:30 p.m. Jiff and I leave Lancey's, separate and I head over to Whit's.

7:40-7:45 p.m. I arrive at Whit's house to find Claudette already there and Justice already gone.

7:40 p.m. Whit is dead when Brandy discovers the body

7:59 p.m. Bed and Breakfast shows Marigny arrive with Mavis waiting.

8:04 p.m. Bas arrives at Bed and Breakfast and takes Marigny off with him after a brief conversation with Mavis.

Jiff stood up going to refill his coffee cup and said, "Whoever killed Whit did it between 7:00 p.m. and when Claudette arrived minutes before you did. It could be Claudette, Marigny, Bas or someone else."

"My money is on someone else. We just have to find out who," I said. "Something does not feel right about this. How can someone have time to kill Whit, shoot him fifteen times, go upstairs, find the safe, open the safe and go back downstairs to pick up the dog before leaving? When Justice gets back inside I want to look at that tag on his collar a little closer."

"It's Sunday, but I'd still like to find Justine before the police get to her. They will scare her into assuming she's a suspect and she'll clam up and not speak to us," Jiff said.

"Justine is the scary one. She could scare the police," I said. "I'd love to watch Detective Taylor question her!"

"I need to talk to her and ask if she is arranging any memorial or burial service," Jiff said ignoring my Taylor remark.

"I thought for sure Justine would have reached out to you or Bas over this. Maybe she hasn't heard yet," I said.

"It's been all over the news," Jiff said.

"Then she must be out of town," I said and dropped my robe to the floor when I stood up. "I'm going to take a shower." As I walked out of the kitchen, I let my nightgown slip to the floor. I wasn't wearing anything under it.

"A shower sounds good," Jiff said as I heard his chair sliding away from the table.

🐈 🐈 🐈 🐈 🐈 🐈 🐈 🐈 🐈 🐈

LATER, BEFORE WE drove to Justine's apartment again

in the French Quarter, I suggested go to the Criminal Court Building and ask security if she had been there over the weekend. Jiff agreed, and we headed to the corner of Tulane Avenue and Broad Street. I waited in the car while Jiff walked into the side entrance where everyone passed through security. Since the building was only open Monday through Friday, a small staff worked weekends in case judges had a session or worked in chambers. Everyone had to sign in and out on weekends.

Fifteen minutes later he was back at the car with no news of a Justine sighting. We were both puzzled, but concluded she must have left town for the weekend. It had to be why she had not contacted someone over Whit's death?

"Funny thing is, the Security Guard said Whit's car been here since Friday morning. The guard saw him drive in alone, no Justine with him," Jiff said.

"I wonder why," I said.

Jiff called his investigator and asked her to find out if Justine took a flight somewhere and when or if she had a return ticket booked.

"I remember Whit telling me she went to college in California and had family in San Francisco. She came to New Orleans to go to Law School," Jiff said to his investigator, Michelle.

"Should we reach out to Hanky and Taylor?" I asked.

"Michelle is a tracker. The woman can find someone fast," he said and looked at me.

As soon as Jiff got back in the car and we started on the way to Justine's apartment his cellphone rang. It was his investigator, Michelle, who had Justine's whereabouts over the weekend with her flight schedule and information on her arrival time back to New Orleans. Justine was arriving at the airport in thirty minutes on a flight from San Francisco. Jiff turned the car around and headed to Kenner, the city where the Louis Armstrong New Orleans International Airport is located.

Kenner is about thirty minutes from downtown New Orleans, if there's no traffic. With traffic it could take thirty-five minutes to two hours. Luckily for us, there's multiple ways to and from downtown to the airport. If one is stuck on I-10, one chooses to remain stuck on I-10, since there are three alternate routes that are far more likely to keep moving.

We took Airline Highway to avoid any issues on I-10 and were at the airport in twenty minutes. By the time we parked and made our way inside, the flight was just touching down. We had to wait for the plane to taxi to the gate, and for passengers to push, shove and struggle with their carryon luggage to deplane.

Justine must have been in business class because she was among the first to come down the terminal to the exit where people or limo drivers waited for their friends, family or clients.

She walked briskly while pulling a wheeled Louis

Vuitton suitcase that matched her shoulder tote. She was wearing a tobacco suede jacket, black pants, a black turtleneck and a Hermes scarf. It seems law clerks make a lot more than I originally thought.

"Justine," Jiff called, and she stopped abruptly, looking around to see who called her.

Justine looked over and scanned the people around us and followed the voice calling her name. "Oh, hi Jiff, Brandy. Who are you picking up here?" she asked as she stopped and looked like she was trying to decide whether to keep walking or wheel her suitcase over toward us.

"Actually, we were looking for you," Jiff said. "Come with us where we can speak more privately, please."

"If this is about Whit, I've made my decision. I can't deal with him anymore," she said shaking her head but following Jiff and I over to the middle of the sprawling seating area adjacent to the airline ticket counters. Jiff found seats together away from other people.

"It is about Whit, but not about your relationship with him," Jiff said. "Where did you go this weekend if you don't mind me asking?"

She hesitated a moment and developed an attitude of *how could this possibly be any of our business* that came across in her voice, not her facial expression. "I flew home to San Francisco to visit my family. I broke off the engagement with Whit and needed some distance from him." She looked back and forth to each of us before asking, "What's this about?"

Justine had only one facial expression, and that one was devoid of all emotion. She was not one to give away secrets or let someone see she was pleased by smiling or displeased by frowning. Her one, stoic expression remained the same the entire time I had known her including now.

Jiff took a deep breath and said, "Whit was murdered in his home on Friday night after you dropped him off."

If I expected Justine to show grief, sadness or perhaps even exuberance for having Whit totally out of her life, I was wrong. I thought about reaching for her hand to comfort her but I didn't for fear of getting frostbite.

"How?" Justine sat ridged on the edge of the lounge chairs with that same stoic expression. She didn't even appear all that interested in who might have done it.

"We're waiting on the Coroner's final report. We were hoping you could help us with who might have wanted him dead," Jiff said.

She sat with an unchanging expression on her face that I took to mean she didn't want to tell us anything.

"It looks like someone tried to get information out of him," Jiff added.

"Jiff let his jacket at Lancey's after you both left so I offered to drop it off to him on my way home. When I got to his house, the door was open and Justice was nowhere to be found. Whit was in his study on the floor. He was already dead," I said.

"We know you dropped him off. Did you go in?" Jiff asked her.

"I broke it off with him on the way to his home from Lancey's. He wanted me to come in and get something to deliver to one of his friends," she said.

"Do you know what he wanted you to deliver and to who?" Jiff asked.

"We didn't get that far. It was the last straw in our relationship. I'm sure it was money. He never had money to pay for anything, dinners, theatre tickets, takeout. He always expected me to pay, and he said he'd pay me back. He never did. I decided to cut my losses," she said.

"Do you have an idea how much money he wanted you to take to someone?" I asked.

"I don't know who he owed the money to, but he had at least one hundred thousand dollars in his bedroom safe. I saw it in there that morning before we left for the courthouse," she said. "I asked him how much money was in there when he opened it that morning to take out some cash. I asked why did he have it in his home and not a bank."

Jiff and I both looked at her nodding to go on.

"He said part was for his son's tuition and some was for a business deal," she said. "Business deal was his code for gambling debts or so I've learned. It was at that moment I decided I had to break it off or be sucked into a never-ending spiral of financial losses. I made airline reservations as soon as I got to my office to leave that evening to visit my family. I didn't tell him until I dropped him at his house that evening after we left Lancey's."

"Do you have any idea who Whit owed it to?" I asked her.

"No. Whit didn't have that much in any of his accounts because he had me do all his record keeping."

"What about the trust fund from his parents?" Jiff asked.

"Trust fund? Never heard about that," Justine never changed her facial expression once since we mentioned Whit was killed except now her eyes got steely.

"Why are you asking about the money? Was he robbed?" she asked.

"It looks that way," Jiff said.

"I didn't need his money. He needed mine," she said as if she expected us to ask. "My family owns several banks and investment firms in California."

"Didn't the police try to contact you? We tried to call you but everything went to voicemail," Jiff said.

"My phone fell out of my purse and is in my car. I didn't miss it until I got on the plane. I was rushing to get to the flight and looked for it when they ask you to turn off any cellular devices. When I couldn't find it, I tried to locate it with the app on my computer. It showed it in the parking lot in the space with my car. I was going to turn it off anyway so I wouldn't be bothered with calls from Whit."

"I'm sure the police will want to speak to you," Jiff said.

"I'll have an attorney if they want to ask me more than what you've asked," she said rummaging in her Louis Vuitton handbag for her keys. Once she found them, she checked her watch before she said, "Tomorrow should be interesting since I need to go into work and see if I still have a job. I hope they let me stay until I find another one."

Justine just told us her family was in banking and Whit needed her money. So why is it when she hears her fiancé was murdered, her first concern is if the courthouse will keep her on until they find a replacement?

"Whit left his jacket at Lancey's on Friday night and I was returning it to him when I found him dead in his office. There was a praline in one of the pockets with Whitmer for Judge on the wrapper. Do you know where he got that?" I asked.

Justine took a moment and said someone made them for Whit's political campaign, one of his friends, maybe. She said it wasn't Whit because he never used his personal money for the campaign.

"One more thing," I said. "What did August and Pierre say to Whit on your way out of Lancey's?"

"I didn't hear the exchange. It was noisy in there and I was worried I'd miss my flight," she said and got up and left. She never shed a tear or even looked dismayed or sad by the news of Whit's murder. Her expression never changed.

🐐 🐐 🐐 🐐 🐐 🐐 🐐 🐐 🐐 🐐

"SHE'S AN ICY one. Do you think she didn't hear what August and Pierre said?" Jiff asked me as Justine rode the escalator to the parking level.

"No, she had to hear them standing right next to Whit. We still need to find out who Whit owed a gambling debt to and how much. Those two from Lancey's would be a good place to start."

Chapter Fifteen

MONDAY MORNINGS AT my office always greeted me with a dozen calls from clients. Three wanted to meet with me to discuss backups to their security systems. Four calls were about suspected hacking and the other calls were miscellaneous questions about billing and installation schedules. While I welcome what this would do for my commission checks, I wanted to research Whit's golfing pals.

I called a staff meeting with the five people who report directly to me and doled out the accounts I wanted reports run on. I asked them to have the preliminary reports on the systems by the time I left for my first afternoon appointment. At least I'd know what they had to upgrade or backup.

After I called everyone back, setting up appointments to meet with those needing face time, I pulled out my files and reviewed the last meetings we had. This took me until lunchtime so I took lunch at my desk. I started doing some basic searches on August Randolph IV and Pierre LeBlanc III. These guys were uptown boys and their families had money. They would definitely circle the wagons as soon as anyone came asking questions if they hadn't already.

Facebook and LinkedIn had nothing on the two men. However, once I Googled them and found their business websites, they all had bios with their marital status, finding names of their wives and children. I searched their wives and their kids' Facebook accounts. Social media showed they belonged to every social organization in the city with a vast display of photos. They both were members of country clubs, yacht clubs and the old-line carnival organizations. Both were in the Knights of Babylon, Krewe of Hermes and the hundred-fifty plus year old Mistick Krewe of Comus.

Pierre LeBlanc's wife probably had a line of credit at Saks' that would rival my annual income. August Randolph was recently widowed and lived just off St. Charles Avenue on Napoleon Avenue. Pierre had an equally enormous home on State Street.

My phone reminder pinged indicating I needed to leave for my first appointment of the day. I had three back-to-back meetings so I wouldn't get back to my research, or 'snooping' as Dante referred to my research, until 4:30 or 5:00 p.m. Hopefully, my meetings would not get too involved or complicated, or worse, rescheduled until later in the day. I planned to go home after my last appointment, feed Meaux and Justice, let them outside to play while searching for more information on Whit's golfing buddies.

My phone rang on my way home. It was from

Dante's personal cell number so I answered, "Hello Dante."

"Hey, I hope I'm not catching you at a bad time," he said.

Uh oh. When did the real Dante ever care about catching me at a bad time?

This could only mean the pod people had Dante along with Julia. That could prove entertaining since their pod selves would be nicer to each other and everyone else.

"No-o-o-o-o, this is a good time," I said wondering what is this about now. "But is this good for you? Don't you have an ongoing investigation?"

I felt we landed in role reversal.

"That's what I have Hanky and Taylor doing. Look, I called to find out if you want to come over and see my place this week."

"Well…maybe, it depends on what day. This week is starting off chaotic," I said.

"What about a late lunch Friday? There's a couple of good places to eat just a block from my house."

"I can't do Friday," I said. "Let's make a tentative plan for lunch on Wednesday if that works for you."

"That works," he said. "Not tentative. Plan on it. I'll pick you up from your office at one o'clock." He hung up before I could contest and tell him I'd meet him.

Some things never change, like his hanging up without saying goodbye. That's how I knew the pod people hadn't gotten him yet. This plan might be OK, I thought. Food is of paramount importance to Dante, so we see his place, then leave and go grab lunch. He won't want to linger there since he'll be hungry. We could see it and leave before he started with any pitiful comments on how this could have been our place together.

This had been a long Monday with one appointment after the next. Some days were like this and I was mentally exhausted at the end. Clients wanted answers fast when it come to their business being hacked or fraudulent activity suspected. Sometimes it took many hours and even days of going over data in different formats to find what was inconsistent.

After sitting with three IT guys all afternoon getting questions answered and collecting batches of data, I had to review it before I delegated it to a member of my team. It had to be someone I trusted to do the same intensive search I do to collaborate my findings.

I wanted to go home, pet my dog, correction, pet my dogs, then have a glass of wine while soaking in a hot bath. Instead, I went back to my office and picked up the data runs so I could look at them tonight at home.

🐈 🐈 🐈 🐈 🐈 🐈 🐈 🐈 🐈

TUESDAY WAS JUST as busy as Monday and my schedule only got more hectic as the day wore on. It became more stressful when I got a text from Jiff.

A search warrant was issued on Bas' home. After the search he was to bring them in for questioning. Jiff said he might not finish until late but would tell me how it turned out. I really needed some free time to search for who might have killed Whit. Neither Jiff nor I believed Bas or Marigny had anything to do with it. The real killer was still out there and probably someone we all knew. He, or she, was letting Bas take the rap.

Every hour I didn't work on the inconsistencies in Whit's scenario to find who else might be the killer just made my stress level escalate. I hunkered down and got my staff in a conference room. I told them we would not be leaving on Tuesday until we identified the issues on my three major accounts. I advised I would order dinner for us if it took that long.

Even though I ran home for lunch and let Meaux and Justice out, I called Suzanne and asked her to take care of my darling fur balls once again.

"Hey, it's me. I need to work late. I went home for lunch and let them out, but I might not get home until 9:00 tonight," I said.

"I always let them out before I leave for work be-tween four and five o'clock. I'll feed them for you. It's no big thing. You realize they will start loving me more than you though, right?" she said.

"No, they won't because most days I run home at lunch and give them a cookie or a piece of cheese," I said. "They know who delivers the good stuff."

"Oh, wait, before you go. A flower arrangement came for you about an hour ago. It's a little on the small side for what Jiff usually sends," she teased.

"Open the card for me, please?" I asked.

"Okay, it's open," she said.

"Well, read it, please. Who signed it?"

"No one signed it," she said. After a very pregnant pause, she said, "It says, *Looking forward to our lunch tomorrow.* Are you stepping out on Jiff?"

"Oh, no. And no, I'm not stepping out on Jiff. Those are from Dante."

"Oh, no," Suzanne said.

"Oh, yes," I said. "This is exactly what I was afraid of."

"You're afraid of lunch or food in general?" Suzanne asked.

"It's not the lunch part. He asked me to go to lunch and look at his new place. It seems he finally moved out of his parents' house and has an apartment. He asked me if I would make suggestions to decorate his place."

"You're gonna help him? Dante?" she asked. "Really?"

"Sure, how hard can it be? I can make it look like his precinct office or a crime scene with tape on the floor suggesting dead bodies have been discovered there. I'll suggest something familiar to him," I said. "I don't have a clue why I'm doing this to help him. I guess I just feel bad for him," I said. My nerves were ratcheting up, and I was craving a piece, no—a whole—King Cake.

"Oh, that's not good. This is how he reels you in,"

she said. "Wait. He wants you to help him select furniture for his new place? You do remember he couldn't help us move? Either time?"

"I can't be that mean to remind him of not helping. He's being so nice now," I said.

"I'll remind him for you," she said. "He's my cousin and he didn't help me either. He wants something. Guess what it is."

"I think he just doesn't know where to start and wants some help," I said.

"He wants back in your good graces, and Jiff out of your life."

"Why don't you come with us? I'll pay for you," I sounded desperate even to myself.

"No, no, no. I'm not getting in the middle of that," she said. "You are on your own. I'll watch the dogs for you anytime, though. What are you going to say about these flowers if Jiff sees them?"

"The truth," I said. "Jiff knows Dante and I have a history growing up next door to each other. I've told him I'm trying to keep it a civil and platonic friendship since we run into each other over dead bodies regularly."

"Flowers don't say platonic," Suzanne said.

"I really don't know how I'm going to handle this. Any ideas? I'm listening," I said.

"Gotta run or I'm going to be late for work," she said and hung up.

"Thanks," I said to the dial tone.

🐐 🐐 🐐 🐐 🐐 🐐 🐐 🐐 🐐 🐐

IT WAS LATE, almost 8:30 p.m. when we took a break and I ordered pizza for my team. I'm not a fan of pizza and my appetite was still off since seeing Whit dead on the floor of his home. We had done as much preliminary planning for systems revisions as possible so we did a recap of what we had on the accounts while we ate. We called it a wrap at 9:30 p.m. I took a few minutes before I left to Google the FindMe app to determine what it was about. It seemed to still be in beta testing. How did Whit get this for Justice?

There were pages of information on testing, government filings, etcetera, etcetera, for the product but no information on how it actually worked. I would have to get on Whit's computer to find out how the beta test was supposed to work that tracked Justice's whereabouts.

Suddenly the timing for having lunch with Dante was looking good. He might even consider letting me have a look at that computer if I had something to exchange or help his case along. If he wouldn't let me, I'd appeal to Hanky.

Hanky and I weren't what you'd call BFFs, but we shared a few moments and she adopted one of my rescues. I could appeal to her common sense and make a case for allowing me to find evidence they might be overlooking. I needed to get Dante to let me see that app on Whit's computer.

Chapter Sixteen

WEDNESDAY AT 12:55 p.m. a text arrived on my phone from Dante saying he was downstairs waiting for me. I texted I'd be right down. I fluffed up my hair, refreshed my lipstick and spritzed my favorite perfume on my wrists and rubbed them together to get the oil to absorb into my skin.

Dante was leaning on the passenger side of an unmarked police car parked at the front door when I walked out of my building. He pushed himself off the car when I approached.

"Shouldn't I follow you in my car? Isn't this a police car? Isn't it for police business? Besides what if you get a call?" I fired off questions trying to find the right one, so he'd agree for me to follow him.

"This is a police car assigned to me twenty-four-seven, and if I get a call, I'll bring you back to your office building. No problem," he said. "But you have to sit in the back behind the screen."

"Wait. What?"

"Just joking," he said ushering me into the front passenger seat.

I didn't want to be held captive by Dante until he was ready to bring me back to work, but I figured I could always call a taxi or Uber.

"Are we eating first or looking at your apartment first?" I asked.

"It's a surprise," was all he would say and smiled.

Uh oh. Dante's surprises were more like shock treatments than anything that resembled a celebration or happy ending. I blamed it on his having looked at so many dead bodies.

Conversation with Dante was usually non-existent, but then, we never spoke much unless Dante was describing his last crime scene. I didn't want to ask him about his last one since we were about to eat lunch. My appetite was returning after seeing Whit dead five days earlier.

Today, Dante was regaling me with the goings on at his new office, what Hanky and Taylor were up to, and not once, did he report on a crime scene.

We pulled up to a camelback shotgun double on a quiet street in the River Bend area where Carrollton Avenue curves and turns into St. Charles Avenue. There are tons of rentals here with Tulane and Loyola Universities along with Loyola's Law School all next to each other across from Audubon Park. It's an upscale college area with lots of places to eat sprinkled in.

His front porch had a wrought iron divider that matched the railings. Dante's side had room for a swing or bistro set should he want to sit out front.

When he opened the front door, I head a familiar voice bellow, "Is that you, Dante? You gots my girl wit ya?"

It was Woozie, and I hadn't seen or spoken to her since her involvement in the proposal fiasco this past Christmas. She had helped trick me into stopping at my parents on the way to Jiff's parents' house where I had planned to spend Christmas Eve.

My Dad, also in the mix, all but carried me next door to see the Deedlers—Dante's parents. There was Dante waiting with his entire family along with mine watching as he kneeled down and offered me a small blue velvet jewelry box. A sensation like a cold hand ran up my back and grabbed me by the throat.

Suddenly—thankfully, Hanky had burst in with a multiple homicide that Dante was being called to by the Chief of Detectives. Off he ran before he actually asked me to marry him. So, I turned and walked out right behind him and Hanky and continued on with my plans for spending Christmas with Jiff.

Now, Woozie grabbed me into her big arms and almost smothered me saying "Oh, Lords" and "I'm so sorry I ever got involved in your business at Christmas." She finished with "Please forgive me and forgive your daddy. He still be sick over it."

"Woozie," I managed to say once I broke free and gasped for air. "Let's move on."

"Lawd, child, you gots to call yo' daddy. He still feels bad about the whole mess, even though your momma still bes mad at you. Yo' daddy misses you."

"Well, my mother's whole purpose in life is to find something and remain mad at me until the end of time. That's nothing new," I said. "I'll call him or go see him. Problem is, she'll be there and I'll have to listen to it."

My mother had left several voicemail messages after I walked out last Christmas Eve. When I turned off the ringer and declined to take the calls, she must have gotten my dear sister to show her how to text so she could continue berating me. I finally blocked her. By now she will have worked herself up to foaming at the mouth if she sees me. Visiting my dad would not be a pleasant visit either because she will have been taking it out on him for how I acted.

"I know, and I feels bad I be partly to blame for putting you in that fix," Woozie said.

"My mother would have found something else to beat me up over. After all it was Christmas, her favorite time to holiday bash me," I said trying to make light of it since Dante was standing right there. "What are you doing here?"

"Uh, uh, sometimes I cleans and…and…sometimes I does the wash," Woozie said wringing her hands. "Yeah, cleans and wash. Here, at Dante's house."

"Clean? There's no furniture," I said looking around.

She hurried to add, "Sometimes I cook. Like today. Dis be your favorite for lunch. Chicken and Dumplings. I gots to run. You and Dante can serve yourselves," she said, and all but flew out the front door.

Wait. What? "Lunch? Here?" I asked Woozie's back going out the front door. Then I turned to look at Dante and asked him, "Lunch here?"

"Surprise!" he said, although it sounded more like "Stop or I'll shoot!"

Dante was moving toward the kitchen where there were two bar stools at the counter dividing the kitchen from the dining and living room areas. There was no table to eat at. Woozie had set the bar with two plates, two forks, two knives, two paper napkins. She seemed to still be trying to push Dante and I together.

On the stove was this massive cast-iron skillet simmering with chicken and dumplings. It was big, old and looked like it had been rescued from a plantation home where it had been put to use making soap or dying clothes. It had to belong to Woozie.

"I thought we were going out to eat," I said trying to figure a way out of this. "You should keep this for your dinner later."

"Woozie wanted to see you to make amends. She figured making your favorite dish would put her back in your good graces. She misses you," he said.

I cringed. Woozie missed me but she just can't help herself and keep her nose out of my business. I missed her, too, if I was being honest.

"Well," I said looking around. "This is a nice place, and big. You could do just about anything here," I said.

"It looks big because it's almost empty," Dante said. "That's why I wanted you here to see it and recommend what I should get."

He had an old sofa that looked like something the fraternities used to move out to the neutral ground or sidewalks to sit on and watch parades, then abandon it there after Mardi Gras. There was, however, a brand-new TV, at least a 70-inch giant screen that looked to be the size of the ones in the Palace AMC Cinemas in the shopping mall.

He sure didn't need me to help pick out electronics, and that was a good thing. The gargantuan TV was sitting on a wooden crate that was stamped with shipping instructions. The crate had a warehouse, protection for its cargo look about it more than a Pier One or World Bazaar thing going on. The two stools at the counter made for his dining space and that was it on the ground floor.

He had the paper shades you buy at the hardware stores for five dollars on the windows for privacy. No curtains. I saw a staircase going up but didn't want to ask to see his bedroom. He probably put all his effort into it and might even have a mirror on the ceiling I did not want to know about.

There was just an overwhelming sad feeling about his apartment and it made me feel sorry for him. Not sorry enough to want to give us another chance, but sorry because I didn't want to.

"So, what do you suggest for down here?" he asked

me. "I've held off getting furniture because I really don't know what to buy. I want it to look like it goes together and not like this—early garage sale. Maybe you can go shopping with me?"

He sounded so sad and his place looked so pitiful I said I could go shopping on Saturday for an hour or two. Then an imaginary slap to the back of my head made me wonder what was I doing. This was classic Dante hooking me back into his world, by appealing to that DNA all women have that makes us feel sorry for the sad, pitiful or abandoned. Dante was not abandoned like one of my rescues and I didn't have to find or save him. Yet, I heard myself saying…

"Well, an area rug would be nice, something light and a coffee table. Why don't you hang your TV on the wall and you don't have to get a TV base cabinet unless you want one," I suggested.

"Maybe I could paint that crate. The landlord doesn't want big holes in the walls," he said.

"Great idea. Paint that crate. That would look better and save you some money. You could use another chair that goes with your sofa," I said. There were five folding beach/lawn chairs leaning against the wall next to the sofa.

When he saw me looking at the folding chair and sofa he said, "I got those chairs for my brothers to come over and watch a game. I want a new sofa and chair. That sofa is temporary. It's been in my dad's garage for the last ten years and I took it to have something to sit on." Dante looked around like he was visualizing new stuff in his place. "I think I also need a picture or two," he added.

Pictures? Like crime scene photos, I wondered to myself.

"Pictures would be nice. Why don't I help you pick out some living room furniture to get you started. You can add to it as you go along. Do you know what kind of sofa you want?"

"I like leather sofas," he said. "What other kinds are there?"

"Leather is nice, but it's a little expensive, although it will last a long time," I said. "There're sectionals, loveseats and sofa combos, or just a long, nice sofa."

"No loveseat. They are too small," he said. "Let's eat and we can talk about it some more."

We served ourselves and we sat across from each other on the countertop. It was easier to talk like this. I nearly exhausted myself asking him what he liked in coffee tables, end tables, and dining room furniture.

"Do you want to see the bedrooms? They're up-stairs," he said.

"I don't want to overwhelm myself thinking about too many rooms and what to recommend. So, let's stay with the living room for now," I said.

"Right, good idea," Dante said.

I finally decided it was time to broach the subject of Whit's computer while he was paying attention to anything and everything I said. We finished our meal, and no one called with a dead body for Dante to rush off and look at. Now was the time to strike with my request.

"You know, Whit never changed any of his pass-words on anything for as long as I've known him. Did your guys get into his computer yet?"

"They were having a little trouble," he said. "Why?"

"Well, I think there's a relatively new program on it that's in Beta testing for locating missing things, like a dog," I said.

"I thought you found the dog," he said.

"I did, but then I thought about this program. I'm pretty sure it records and tracks the path or direction the dog went," I said. Now, I noticed the vein on the side of his head began pulsating like it does when I'm telling him something he doesn't want to hear.

"Look, this might find the real killer. I could give it to Jiff and his team defending the judge first," I said.

"He'll find it out anyway if you give it to me," he said.

"Yes, but he's only interested in clearing Judge Martin and his daughter. He's not interested in finding out who killed Whit," I said, "I mean he'd like to find out who killed Whit but his priority differs from yours. His priority is the judge and the daughter. So, be the hero. It doesn't hurt to do a solid for a judge," I finished.

Dante looked like he was going over the scenarios in his head while the vein slowly stopped pulsating.

"What is it you think you can find out on that computer?" he asked.

"I need to look at the app and see if it tracked the path the dog took after leaving Whit's house. It could have a history that shows a stop or something to suggest who took the dog from the house and dumped him at the shelter. I'm hoping the murderer's car has or stored something like a GPS path back to a home address we could combine with the FindMe GPS off the application."

"Then we put the two together and that should lead to the killer?" he asked leaning forward over his empty plate.

"Maybe, then you could get a warrant for someone's car and see if their GPS tracks with the one on the dog's collar to the shelter. It's a long shot, but that would tie the dog to whoever took him from Whit's house, and it might show who followed Whit home."

"What makes you think someone followed him?" he asked.

"Because, the window of opportunity to kill him was tight, and the people who went in and out of Whit's house I spoke to didn't see his dog, or each other. Remember, I said to look at the bloody paw prints around the body? They didn't run away from the body, only around it. It seems as if whoever killed Whit picked up Justice and took him to avoid attention being drawn to the barking and someone coming over to check on him."

"Taylor and Hanky also thought someone took the dog, but since you found him at the shelter tied to a fence, that was a dead end." He rubbed the vein on the side of his head. It bulged, but not as bad.

"That's why it's important. Anyone who didn't care about the dog or dogs in general, would have dumped him in someone's neighborhood on their way home," I said. "It sounds like someone who knew Whit, someone who knew his pass codes, someone his dog knew and assumed he'd be home alone."

"Well, there was no forced entry, and we didn't find the dog," he said. He added, "You did."

I knew Dante's resolve was weakening anytime he resorted to flattering or complimenting me. It was a skill he rarely used, and he wasn't very good at it.

"So, can I have a look at the computer to see if it tracked the dog? I'll tell you whatever I find, and you might be able to get a warrant for the GPS in the real killer's car," I said smiling.

"When do you want to do this? And, you can only look at that app," he said.

"What about now? Can you take me to the tech working on it?" I asked in my sweetest voice.

"You know I can't do that," Dante said.

"I could just hack into his computer since I know all his passcodes from years of his not changing them," I said.

"Then I'd have to arrest you," he said.

"You would arrest me when I might help you find

the murderer? I don't think so," I said. "I don't know why this is so hard for you. Most people accept help when and where they can get it—free of charge, I might add."

Dante slammed his hand down on the counter, and with a bulging vein on the side of his head said, "Come on. I'll drop you at your car and you can meet me at the precinct. I'll register you as a consultant."

Chapter Seventeen

I RAN HOME to let the Meaux and Justice out before heading to meet Dante. Suzanne was home but upstairs, sleeping or studying, so I left her a note saying I had been home and what time the dogs were last out. I told them I'd take them for a long walk this evening after I got home. They stood watching me leave with a pensive gaze that meant they would not forget about the promise of an outing.

AT THE PRECINCT I asked for Dante and was escorted back a long hall with a dozen doors off in either direction before we came to one marked 'Evidence.' The uniformed escort knocked on the door and Dante opened it to let me in leaving my escort outside.

There were three lab techs sitting in front of desks working with their heads and shoulders slumped over their computers. Dante stood next to a man with a head of dark wavy hair, and an acne pockmarked face. His stubby fingers punched the keyboard of his computer with the enthusiasm of a mafia hit man trying to get information out of someone.

His oversized frame spilled over the sides of his office chair where he was sitting in front of a computer. He looked to be a few cannoli shy of three hundred pounds. The seams and buttons of his uniform were screaming for release from the perpetual torture of being stretched. He did not glance up when I entered the room. The two on the opposite side of the workspace did. I exchanged nods of acknowledgment with them and their eyes returned to their screens.

Dante cleared his throat as if trying to get the giant man's attention before saying, "Ozzie, have you had any luck getting into Judge Whitmer's computer?"

Ozzie answered by shaking his head no and not looking away from his computer screen.

"Well, this is Ms. Alexander, a consultant who might be able to access the passcodes on Judge Whitmer's computer. Can you set her up at it, please?" Dante asked him ignoring how rude Ozzie was being.

"Hi, nice to meet you Ozzie," I said. The hair on my neck started to tingle and I suppressed a shudder from going up my back.

Ozzie didn't answer but pushed back from the desk he was working at in his rolling chair. While he remained seated, he walked it over to one of the file cabinets lining an entire wall on the other side of the twelve by twelve room. He opened the middle drawer and removed a computer.

I wondered if he ever stored anything in the top two filing cabinet drawers because that meant he would have to stand up to reach or see what was inside. I guessed the top two filing drawers were for the other two techs on the other side of his desk to use. Then, he chair-walked back to another desk and pointed to an open chair for me to sit at.

There were power strips on the tops of all the desks so Ozzie or anyone working on computer stuff never had to bend over to plug something in or unplug it.

"It's ready," Ozzie said after the laptop appeared to have powered up.

"Thanks, Ozzie," Dante seemed to say to no one since Ozzie did not seem to be listening, Dante was talking more to Ozzie's back now that he had shoved off and rolled back to his original position he started in.

Dante searched and found a chair. He pulled up next to mine and sat down to watch me.

I logged in and tried the 007 password Whit used since the beginning of time. Next, I tried his favorite number which was his birthday along with his best golf score, 11 11 73. November 11, and his golf score was 73. The numbers worked. I was in.

Once logged into his computer I searched for the FindMe application. I logged in with the same password along with Whit's email.

The FindMe file was named Justice with his smiling doggy face as his avatar. The application listed every route, by date and time ever taken by Justice. It also logged the distance travelled and his whereabouts at this very moment. Wow! I wanted one of these for

Meaux.

I clicked on the date Whit was murdered and Justice's route popped up. That morning Whit took him on a walk around the block, and the first route that day was a spaghetti track taken, all within the perimeter of Whit's house. The next route showed Justice leaving Whit's house at 7:36 p.m.

"Dante, this shows the tracker stopped in two places," I said. "This assumes the dog was in a car by now. This track shows the dog leaving Whit's house and traveling around the corner stopping mid-block. Then it drives over to St. Charles Avenue, stops for a minute and proceeds to the West Bank Animal Shelter. Whose car is this and who took the dog with them?"

I assumed the stops were for the driver to talk on the phone or look up something, like the shelter's address.

"Yeah, well, what are those addresses? Can you tell?" Dante asked.

"Let me see. This app is pretty awesome. It shows a lot of detail," I said.

"Except for the license plate of the car or a photo of the driver," he said.

"What would be the fun in that? This might tell us the address of the driver's home if he stopped there," I said. The two techs working on the other side of the desk from Ozzie got up and left.

"We can't be that lucky," Dante said.

I played with a few more keys and looked around in

the app and clicked on the route. It showed the exact times the car stopped and in front of what address. "Neither address belongs to the two golfing buddies Whit owed money to. Are there cameras on the street or on someone's home that caught a photo of the car and driver?" I asked.

"I'll send out detectives to canvas the area. Most home security systems only pick up movement and activity close to the home. Rarely are they sophisticated enough to catch a license plate or driver. We're lucky we see a car in them. Faces need to look directly into the camera, and most home invaders know where they are and avoid them."

I noticed that there was no sound coming from the direction of Ozzie—no grunting, no punching his keypad, no chair walking from point to point in the room. When I stopped moving around on the screen, I tapped Dante on the arm and pointed behind me toward Ozzie who sat listening. Dante held up a finger as if to wait a moment.

There was dead silence for a few moments before Ozzie asked, "Finding anything?"

"Well," I said. Dante put his hand on my arm to stop me from saying anything else so I added, "Not really." When I looked around, Ozzie's back was to us, but he was sitting straight up in his chair listening. His hands were poised in the air over his keyboard. Well, if he wanted to eavesdrop, I'd give him an earful.

I looked at Dante and moved my eyes to my hand

where I had taken a sleek gold drive out of my pocket. I came prepared with a drive that could hold at least a two Terabytes of data. He nodded, indicating it was okay for me to use it. I slipped the drive into the USB port on the side of Whit's computer and said for Ozzie's benefit, "Let's see what else this application can tell us." I moved the application onto the flash drive along with all of Whit's emails, all the files in his documents folder and all his photos.

"The judge sure has a lot of dog photos in this app to ID Justice if he got lost." I continued to copy any files that deemed worthy of a closer look. I rattled on how cute Justice was in his sweaters, numerous matching collars and leashes. I had to make Ozzie think we were just wasting time until I finished copying what I wanted, deleted the photo file, ejected the drive and nodded at Dante. I deleted the photo file and emptied the trash folder. When I removed the thumb drive, I put it down the front of my blouse into my bra so Ozzie wouldn't see anything in my hand.

"Well, dog photos aren't going to help us," Dante said. "Are you done?"

"Yes, I'm not sure this helps you or not. It doesn't really give you any concrete evidence," I said.

"Thanks for trying," he said. "Ozzie, do you mind putting this back. We'll turn it off and unplug it."

Ozzie ignored us again for the second time.

As WE WALKED back to his car, I asked, "What's your

take on Ozzie?"

"Why do you ask?" Dante said.

"Because he was less than helpful, didn't speak, lacked common courtesy to answer when spoken to. He also listened to everything we said."

"I noticed that," he said.

"Why did you let me take a copy of the computer files?" I asked.

"In case that file goes missing from that computer," he said flatly. When I looked at him in disbelief, he added, "It happens. I need that flash drive."

"Can I have one more peek at it? You can come up to my office and I'll be just a minute. Maybe I can figure out the exact addresses the car stopped in front of." I said. I already knew the exact addresses the car stopped in front of, but I wanted a copy of that drive. "Whoever took the dog is the killer, but as soon as he left the dog at the shelter the tracking stopped."

"Yes, I figured that, but someone's car will match the route up to the drop-off at the shelter."

"Exactly. All newer model cars have GPS or that OnStar systems to track where they are, and where they've been. Seems you need a warrant for a vehicle you believe belongs to the killer," I said.

"Yes. I'll start with Judge Martin and his daughter," Dante said.

"You still think they did it? Really?"

"It will tell us one way or the other," he said. "Could possibly clear him."

"Well, it clears his daughter who walked to Whit's house and then called an Uber to take her to her mother at the guest house."

"Yes, I think she's cleared also, but the two of them have something to hide, don't you think?" he asked me.

My hand flew to my chest to check my heart rate. Was Dante really asking for my opinion?

"Yes, but why do you think that?" I asked.

"Because you could see on the video from the guest house, the daughter gave her mother something. She had just come from Whit's. Don't you wonder what that something is?" he asked and took a side look at me.

I'm not good at lying. Dante figured out that I knew what it was. I said, "I can only take a guess which might be wrong. I don't want to cast a shadow on Marigny or her mother on a guess."

"So, you know what it is," he said.

"Are you interrogating me?"

"Only if you are withholding vital information," he said giving me one of the most charming smiles I have ever seen on Dante's face.

"Well…" I said, "If I were you, I'd look at the photos on this flash drive and you might find something. You might also think long and hard before you do anything with those photos. I have an idea of what they are from what Claudette told me the night Whit was murdered, and we waited for the police to show up."

"Porn?" Dante said.

"Why is your first guess always porn?"

"Because it's more likely porn than cat videos," he said.

"I hate it when you're right," I said. "You need to be especially prudent with those photos. If it is what you think they are or something close to it, then someone could be publicly embarrassed and ruined if they came out. You should consider their influence on the people involved and whether it actually solves or is evidence in this case," I said. I hesitated before I added, "I deleted all the photos of the porn off the computer at the station."

Dante slammed a flat hand on the roof of his vehicle raising his voice at me to say, "Why did you do that? You are tampering with evidence."

"No, because it's right here," I said patting the front of my blouse where the drive was hidden. I started talking fast, "I don't know if the photos have anything to do with Whit's death other than someone wishing he was dead if they ever came out. Clayton Haines, does not seem to be on your radar, or the missing money from his safe."

"Brandy…" he said trying to interrupt me so he could yell some more.

"Besides, you were the one who said you thought the info on that computer could go missing. What if the information that could clear them disappears and photos that could embarrass them get leaked? How would it reflect on you, your officers and how does it affect your investigation then?"

That shut him up.

The area around the precinct was in one of the worse parts of the city for crime. Dante's car was parked at the corner and just as he opened the driver's side car door a white van reeled around the corner. Someone on the passenger side, wearing a ski mask, stuck an arm out and hit Dante with a Taser. I was about to scream when the passenger sliding door opened at the same time and a man in a ski mask jumped out and hit me with one as well.

Chapter Eighteen

WHEN I CAME to and opened my eyes, it was pitch black. In fact, it was so dark I blinked to make sure my eyes were open. They adjusted to see a dim glow next to my head.

Dante patted my face to get me to come to. I was lying on what felt like rubble—lumpy, wet, and hard. My hand discovered a concrete floor when I tried to sit up. I frantically felt around either side of me for my purse.

"Ooooh, my head hurts…what…happened?" Somebody must have slugged me.

"Someone hit us with a Taser stun gun," he said.

"Who would do that?" I pushed up on my elbow rubbing my head. "Did he hit us in the head with it too?"

"Seems like it. Probably after they got us in the van," Dante said.

Dante was sitting with his legs straight out and I had been lying on my back with my head in his lap in pitch black darkness. Only a dim glow came from his cellphone on the ground next to him.

"Where's my purse?" I asked and tried to sit up.

"You've been knocked out with a Taser and we're sitting God knows where, and you are worried about your purse?" he asked.

"Where are we?" I asked. I rubbed my head. I had a massive throbbing headache.

"If I had to guess, we're underground somewhere under the casino or along the wharf by the river. Remember where the old Rivergate was?" he said.

"Yeah," I said and tried to sit up.

"Anyway, I'm sure we're under it in one of those tunnels the city dug in the 1960s."

"New Orleans has underground tunnels? How is that possible if we are below sea level?"

"Yes, we have tunnels. Some Einstein politician thought it would be a great idea to have an underground Interstate to drive in and out of downtown so they dug these in the sixties." Dante helped me sit up.

"Wouldn't they fill up with water and then everyone would have to use submarines to drive in and out of downtown?" I asked.

"Some have water in them, but explains why the streets are collapsing like the recent section on Canal, remember?" he said.

"Wait. What? I remember a big sinkhole in front of the Marriott," I said running my fingers through my hair and looking around in the darkness for my purse. "Have you seen my purse?"

"That wasn't a sinkhole. It was one of these tunnels

collapsing from structures made of steel and left underground in New Orleans for the last sixty years—neglected," he said.

"My purse?"

"There's something over there that looks like a bag," he said nodding off into the darkness. "Did you put that thumb drive in your purse?"

"No. The thumb drive is right here," I said reaching into my blouse and retrieving it from the safe place I left it, right in the middle front of my bra. I showed it to Dante then I put it back in its safe place.

As my eyes adjusted, I saw it with most of the items I had in my purse spread out around it.

"The guys who took us might have looked through your purse to see if you had a drive," he said. "This happened close on the heels of us leaving the station."

"I wonder if my cellphone will work," I said.

"Why do you think mine is just a flashlight at the moment? There's probably too much steel, correction, rusting steel down here blocking any reception," Dante said. He stood up, holding his phone at arms-length in all directions trying to find bars to transmit. "Besides whoever dumped us down here figured we'd use the flashlight and run out of battery before we ever make it out of here."

I found my cellphone and sure enough, no bars, no signal, no connection to anything. After turning off all the applications to save my battery, I turned on my flashlight.

"Hey, I also have a flashlight that looks like a lip-stick somewhere in this purse...here," I said holding it up. It was one of my small, LED type with a long battery life. "I bought this as part of my survival kit."

"You bought a lipstick survival kit?"

"It's a flashlight disguised as a lipstick so a kidnap-per won't take it away from you," I told him somewhat pleased with myself.

"I don't think kidnappers worry about lipstick flashlight," he said. "Weren't you a scout as a kid? Like a Camp Fire Girl or a Blue Bell or whatever they're called?"

"Blue Bell is an ice cream company. You're think-ing of the Blue Birds, but I was a Brownie in the Girl Scouts. Our motto was 'Always Be Prepared'. I could have been more prepared by being more observant of our surroundings on the way to wherever we were now."

"I should have been," he said and his shoulders slumped.

"That requires us to be conscious," I said. "Check out this little flashlight. It has some candle power."

"It does. Let me see that," Dante said.

"No, I'll hold on to it," Dante was always trying to get things away from me since we were kids and once he had it, I didn't get it back. "Why are we here?" I finally asked Dante.

"Well, the guys who grabbed us could have killed us. Instead, they left a note in my pocket," he said handing me a piece of paper.

"They left a note? Are you kidding me? Well, wait, that makes sense. There's no cell reception so they couldn't call us, right?" I said reading the typed message in the cellphone/flashlight glow Dante handed me.

STAY OUTTA ANYTHING TO DO WITH THE DEAD JUDGE.

"Hmm. Typed. Classy. The bad guys have access to a computer and a printer," I said. "Their printer could use toner. This suggests we'll find our way out of here. Why not just kill us?"

"I'm a cop, remember? Most, not all, but most bad guys, except for psychopaths have second thoughts about killing a cop. But...it's more likely they didn't kill us because it's hard to get rid of a body, let alone two."

"Well, they got rid of the two of us, here, in this place, and we could easily be just as dead," I said. "This isn't what I'd call a high traffic zone."

"I was starting to come to when one of these guys hit me again. I'm sure it looked like the two of them were helping two drunks," he said. "I didn't see either one of their faces."

"So, maybe that means the entry or exit they brought us in through is close by. You were already awake, right? They wouldn't carry us farther than they had to."

"I remember they moved us on something. It felt

like we slid down something, like a trash chute used at construction sites. I wasn't able to pay attention since they zapped me pretty good. They may have put blindfolds on us, I can't be sure."

"All right. Someone who has serious psychopathic tendencies grabbed us and dumped us in this place. Why take the two of us?" I asked; we were both quiet for a few minutes thinking. "A lot of people saw us together in the precinct looking at Whit's computer. Someone dropped a dime on us, and it has to be one of those three in the computer room. They knew we went to the Evidence Room and looked at that computer, but only one seemed interested."

"I will find who it is and make him sorry he was ever born," Dante said.

"My money is on Ozzie. He made my skin crawl while we were around him. I'm all for you wanting to strangle who is responsible, but could you put that further down on your To Do list. We need to stay calm and focus on the issue at hand—finding a way out of here. These tunnels can't be very deep underground or they would have flooded." I took a step without looking first with the flashlight and landed on all fours in a puddle of filthy water.

"Well, Splash," Dante thought calling me this was hilarious as he helped me to my feet. "I suggest you take it a little slower and watch where you're walking."

"Funny," I said. "I hope this tunnel doesn't flood."

"It seems they might succumb to water intrusion.

These tunnels might flood when the tide comes in. I seem to remember they were built as a six-lane underground highway leading in and out of downtown. Hopefully, they are on one level."

I thought I would have a heart attack thinking about getting trapped in this tunnel, in the dark, in water with God knows what living and crawling around down here. My body started to shake uncontrollably.

"Are you cold?" Dante asked.

"No, just thinking about being trapped in a flooded, dark tunnel with…with…whatever lives in here."

"I'm sorry. I didn't mean to scare you."

"It's okay," I said shaking my head and wringing out my skirt that soaked up the puddle. "Let's check the ceilings in either direction and the walls for an exit. There could be an opening under a building or up to the street. I'll use my survival lipstick flashlight with the LED. It's stronger and we can see better. Let's save the cellphones until we find a spot where we get reception."

"Okay. I'll hold the flashlight," Dante said holding out his hand.

"Why? It's my flashlight. I'm perfectly capable of holding it and pointing it at the ceiling or in any direction. I'm keeping it."

"All right but stay close to me. I don't want you falling again and hurting yourself," he said. He put his hand over my hand holding the light.

We made our way slowly, careful where we stepped for fear there might be holes, rotten areas of the foundation or places left unfinished. The area we walked through was very wet.

Out of the blue, or in this case, out of the darkness, Dante said, "All I ever wanted was to spend the rest of my life with you."

"It looks like you might get your wish, only it's not going to be a very long life if we don't find a way out of here," I said.

Dante moved my hand to shine the flashlight in either direction in the tunnel. The beam never bounced back off the far end of the tunnel.

"Any idea what time it is?" I asked. I slowly picked my way over the trash, debris and odd scraps of wood, rebar and abandoned broken tools, buckets and construction equipment. We stopped to rummage through the tools to see if something was usable in case we found an exit. There was nothing.

"Here, point that thing at my wrist," he said. "It's 9:45 p.m. When we came to, I looked at the time on the phone and it was 6:50 p.m. We left the station at about six or six-fifteen. We've already been down here almost three hours."

"If it was daytime, we might see a light through all of those cracks in the ceiling. Maybe even a streetlight if we're lucky."

"I haven't heard any street noises at all," he said. "Wait. What was that?"

We both stopped and listened.

"Could be the local residents," I said.

He shook his head no and pointed to his ear.

It vaguely sounded like a ship's horn only miles away. There were always ships on the river. They came in or out of New Orleans or on their way up the Mississippi.

"The only way that will rescue us is if he rams into the wharf and busts open this tunnel. Then we'd have to be really lucky to escape without being crushed or drowned," I said and started to shake again.

"We're going to get out of here," he said and patted my hand.

We made our way carefully along the tunnel, taking a step or two then stopping to look up and around for any sign of an exit. The ground was littered with all kinds of debris and when we stepped on any of it, I could hear the scurrying sound of the tunnel dwellers.

"I hope we don't run into any of those sewer rats," I said. "Have you seen the size of those things? They are bigger than my Meaux! They're black with yellow eyes, a slanted head and wet looking. They look prehistoric," I said with an involuntary shudder. I checked the area around my feet with the light every few steps.

"You know, that note bugs me. The fact that we're still alive suggests these guys aren't pros. Maybe whoever killed the judge didn't really want or plan to kill him. They could have gone there for something and he wouldn't give it up and things turned ugly," Dante said. "People get desperate when they're backed in a corner."

"He was full of bullets," I said.

"Yes, but small caliber bullets, the kind used to cause pain and make someone talk," he said. "Bullets from a small gun which are found littering the streets."

"Well, could that have been a soldier working for Clayton Haines in prison?" I asked.

"Seems as if someone wanted the police to think it was Clayton Haines, but the scene was too neat," he said. "I gave the Haines crime family a good, hard look. When the Haines gang commits violence, it's with a lot of wreckage and carnage. They are hateful and destructive. The judge's house was too clean. Also, they haven't pulled a home invasion like this. Their M.O. is to lie in wait somewhere the victim will pass or walk by. They can jump them and pull them behind a convenience store or building and empty fifteen bullets in them against a wall."

"How many bullets did the coroner find in Whit?" I asked.

"That's just it. There were fifteen bullets in Whit but there were at least five more bullets found all over the room. The Haines gunman has never wasted a single bullet of the fifteen he puts in someone. He also used a larger caliber pistol. That gunman is credited with twenty-six kills, and now he gets sloppy? No, not the Haines gang."

"That's why I think it has everything to do with the missing money," I said.

"What missing money?" Dante asked holding his

cell light between us pointing up. We looked like ghouls in the dark by the light of the phone facing each other.

"The money I've mentioned to you before. The money that should have been in his safe according to Claudette. She said Whit was supposed to have his son's tuition in there. There could have been more than tuition money missing from that safe," I said.

"How do you know money was missing and it wasn't empty to begin with?"

"Well, Claudette went there thinking Whit had it and then Jiff and I spoke to Justine on Sunday. She says she was out of town, by the way and we caught her coming off a flight at the airport. Seems she left after she dropped Whit home on Friday," I said. "The Moutons, the neighbors across the street told me she dropped him off and then drove away. Mr. Mouton saw her. She didn't get out of the car."

"Well, that doesn't clear her as a suspect," Dante said. "She could have doubled back."

"Let me finish, you might see it as she had nothing to do with the murder. She said she planned to break it off with Whit after the party when she dropped him at home and went directly to the airport. She had a roundtrip ticket over the weekend to San Francisco."

"Great, there goes my key suspect."

"Justine said she saw a lot of money in that safe the morning he was killed. Before you ask the next question…she asked Whit how much and what was it for. She managed all his accounts, or thought she did. She seemed miffed or maybe she looked irritated, I can't tell with Justine. She didn't know the particulars on where the money came from or where it was going. She said it didn't come from any of the accounts she managed."

"So?"

"So, Claudette told me the money was from a trust fund Whit's parents had for their grandsons' tuition. They gave Whit power of attorney to manage it. Bad move leaving money in the hands of a known gambler. One son is in and out of rehab but the other one goes to private schools," I said.

"How much was it?"

"Justine said Whit told her it was one hundred thousand dollars—ten thousand was for tuition. Whit also told her the rest was for a business deal…his code name for a gambling debt."

I knew he was thinking the same thing I was, and that is, follow the money. He stopped and suggested we take a five-minute break.

"It was all in cash, according to Justine. Impossible to follow," I said.

"Great," Dante said. "I thought it might be a break."

While we both sat in silence. I knew by now Jiff would miss me and be worried about what happened. He would look for me.

The going was slow in the tunnel with so much

debris to step around and over. In some places it was wet and slippery. We didn't want to fall, hurt ourselves and have no way to get help.

Dante could have been reading my thoughts because he stood up and offered his hand to help me up. "I won't let you get hurt down here. I'm going to make sure." When I stood up, his arm went around my waist and he held me tight against him.

While having him hold on to me didn't seem awkward, in fact, I felt safer. I always felt safe with Dante, even when I wasn't completely frustrated or annoyed with him for leaving me to run off and meet someone else—usually a dead body. I know, call me difficult. To break the silence, I told him I spoke to Mavis at Julia's Bed and Breakfast.

"Mavis told me Whit called her the night Justine dropped him off and left. She told him she was getting a massage at her spa when she really was at the B&B. She was still angry with him over everything that happened. She said he sounded pitiful and he told her Justine left him. She said she didn't want him back."

"Did she know Whit's gambling pals?" Dante asked.

"Mavis said they were his golfing buddies," I said.

"If we find out who the last foursome was, and he owes one of them, maybe that's who killed him," Dante said.

"Before you get really excited over who the golf pals are, Bas Martin and Jiff have played with Whit. Let me just say that Bas Martin seems to be a convenience fall guy, so keep that in mind," I said.

"Ah, again, Bas Martin makes an appearance," Dante said pushing a dilapidated, refrigerator-size, cardboard box out of our way with his foot while never letting go of my waist. "I'm just not that lucky for it to be Richie Rich."

I ignored his comment regarding Jiff. I could have told him I was already following this line of thought, but hey, it's not my job and I only wanted to see the murderer caught and clear Bas and his daughter, Marigny. "Mavis told me Whit normally played golf with Bas, and two other guys who have all been friends since LSU. One is now a cardiologist named Pierre LeBlanc, and the other one is a real estate developer named August Randolph. Others drifted in and out but they were the usual foursome.

"You might remember Randolph's dad is big into real estate and always in the newspaper involved in big investment deals in the city. His dad developed the old Rivergate where Harrah's Casino is now. August inherited it all. Mavis said August didn't let money owed to him or debts ride. She said Whit often lost bets to those two and owed them money," I said.

We plodded along for what felt like hours and I was getting hungry. Dante was a three-squares a day man, so I'd bet my next paycheck he was starving. When he was hungry, he got cross. I was also tired, but I did not want to lie down or sit still and have whatever else was living down here touch me, crawl over me or bite me.

The sound of cellophane crunching beneath one of our feet made me stop and shine my light on it.

"I think I found the snack bar, or vending machine," I said with my light on some candy wrappers. "Well, what do we have here?" I fixed my light on several praline wrappers, minus the pralines, with *Whitmer for Judge He's sweet on justice* clearly visible on them.

"Dante, look at this," I said picking a wrapper up. "This is the same praline in the same wrapper as the one I found in Whit's coat pocket the night I found him dead in his study. Coincidence?"

"I don't believe in coincidences," he said taking it from me with the tips of two fingers and picking up the others the same way. "If we get out of here, this might lead us to whoever kidnapped us. This wrapper doesn't look like it's been here long," Dante said inspecting it under the flashlight beam. He carefully folded them trying to only touch the ends and put them in his shirt pocket.

"Well, well, well," I said. "Look at this." I held the light close to the wrapper where the ends would cross together and meet to seal in the praline. In tiny print on the edge of the cellophane, was *Randolph Companies, LLC*. "Look who had these made for Whit's campaign when he ran for judge about a year ago. I'd say these wrappers haven't been here more than a year, if that," I said. "You know what else?"

"What?"

"I bet that wrapper isn't far from an exit to this tunnel," I said.

"I hope you're right. Do you think Whit had been down here?" Dante asked.

"I don't know, maybe. I suspect one of his buddies who has an interest in these tunnels was. One of his buddies is in the Ozzie information network," I said.

"Ozzie? As in Ozzie from the Evidence Room? The guy we who didn't say a word?" Dante asked.

"It's the only Ozzie we both know, and I bet he has a lot to say for the right price," I said.

"I hope you're wrong. That's a big step over the line," Dante said.

"Can we stop again?" I asked him. "I'm in need of a five- or ten-minute break. I need to sit down. It's hard going in these high heels and it feels like we've been plodding along for hours."

"Yeah," he said looking around and pushing debris away to clear an area. "It's almost midnight, so we have been at this for hours."

"And it's past my bedtime," I said.

I stomped my feet around a minute before I sat down next to him with our backs to the wall.

"What are you doing?" he asked.

"I'm just shooing away from us anything that crawls around in this area."

We sat there in silence for a minute and then he put his arm around me and I put my head on his shoulder.

Chapter Nineteen

WE MUST HAVE dozed off because I jumped to my feet when I felt something brush against my leg. I reached around looking to grab onto Dante. Using my free hand with the flashlight I must have looked like a search beacon slicing through the darkness like a laser. "Was that a rat? I hope it was a rat and not a...a..."

"You would rather it be a rat?" he asked as he got to his feet.

"Yes. Yes, a rat. Most definitely, a rat." I cast my light wildly in all directions around my feet, then up the walls and all over the ceiling, then back down to the ground by my feet again. "You know my roach phobia."

"Well...I've seen a million..."

"Don't say it! Don't you even think it! Don't say you saw one if you don't want me to pass out, or hyperventilate, or have a nervous breakdown, or, or, or..."

"It was a rat," he said flatly. "Rats, I've only seen rats." He reached around me and put his hand over mine holding the flashlight to steady it. He stilled the light pointing it down the tunnel in the direction we needed to head.

"Okay, then," I said trying to control the hyperventilating that started. I was a bit self-conscious about the way Dante was holding my hand but I realized I was holding his back, maybe even squeezing it. I had to redirect my thinking away from what could be in the darkness next to me. God help us both if something flew and landed on one of us—well…on me.

"I just don't want to die down here in total darkness, where nobody knows where we are with…with…with…bugs crawling all over me." I checked my clothes, arms, feet and all around where I stood. I shook uncontrollably, like a body shiver that wouldn't stop. "I don't mind the rats."

This might have had more to do with the thought of a single roach crawling over or touching me, than being eaten by rats. Not even starvation, dying in darkness or rats bothered me that much. Roaches. I really hated roaches.

This phobia was thanks to my mother. She used to threaten to put a roach on me when I was a child if I didn't take a nap, didn't eat my dinner, didn't sit still, and on and on. What can I say? She's a whack job, and she almost made me one.

Get a grip, I thought to myself. We have to keep our heads about us if we have any chance of getting out of here.

Dante held my hand and gently guided me to walk along, slowing making our way over all kinds of trash, debris and broken concrete. When my heel caught on a piece of rebar stuck in the ground, Dante grabbed me to keep me upright, preventing a fall. As he steadied me so I could regain my balance I turned to thank him and that's when he kissed me. I let him.

"I will get you out of here if it's the last thing I do," he said when our lips parted.

I wanted to kiss him back for all the years we had known each other. For all the times he took up for me on the playground at school. For all the dates we never had together. And for fear that this might be the last of us. Then, I started laughing.

"What is so funny? Are you delirious or do I kiss that bad?" he asked.

"None of the above. It's just that this is the longest date we've ever had, and it will probably be our last," I said. "We started at lunch, went to the precinct and now it's past our bedtime and we could spend the night in here, or the rest of our lives."

"You're right. Now that you mention it, this is the longest date we've ever had. Are you having a good time, or what?" he asked and he started laughing.

"I know you will get us out of here," I said. "You will get us *both* out of here."

A strange look came over his face and he put a finger to his lips. Then he tapped his ear. We stood listening. There was the sound of gushing water, then what sounded like an engine revving before sounding like it was thrown in reverse.

The fear of the tunnel flooding came rushing back to me. When Dante felt me shiver, he held me tighter.

"That sounds like a ferry or The Natchez river boat," he said. "I think we're close to one of the ferry or riverboat landings. If that's the case, we should try to get someone's attention if we had something to make noise with."

"Wait. What if the guys who left us here work for the ferry or at the ferry landing and are waiting for us to get out? Why aren't we hearing people sounds, like voices, or even car engines?" I asked in a whisper.

"I don't think we are near where we woke up, and that's probably where they dropped us in here," he said.

"Do you think we should go back to where we think they left us?" I asked.

"No. I didn't see any access around us while we were there."

"I think we need to look up more. The sound seems like it's coming from above us. There's been nothing along the walls. There might be an access like a drain cover or electric access point for maintenance," I said pointing the light at the ceiling.

"Good idea," he said. "If it's the ferry or a riverboat, the ramps are long and usually extend past the rear of the boat. I think a maintenance entry would likely be away from where people board."

We made our way along the tunnel listening for

anything to indicate there might be someone to hear us if we made a noise. We were walking carefully with the light pointed to the ceiling of the tunnel. That's when I saw it.

"Dante, look." I said holding the light on a square section cut into the ceiling. "It looks like a rusted hatch cover." I felt excited at the first possibility of escape.

"God, it looks like it's rusted shut," Dante said.

"Well, that's not the positive feedback I was hoping for. First, let's see if we can reach it. It's kinda high up there," I said. Looking back and forth at Dante and the height difference to the hatch I figured it could be about five or six more feet. "The tunnel height appears to be fifteen feet. I guess if it was supposed to be a highway, they took into consideration for the height of delivery trucks to get in and out of the French Quarter."

We both stood trying to figure out how to get one of us up there when I shown the light down the wall and Voila! There was a rusting metal ladder attached to the wall right under the hatch. Could we be this lucky?

"That looks pretty rusted also," I said as Dante grabbed the sides with both hands to hoist himself up. Instead of hoisting himself up, the ladder fell off the wall into his hands causing him to stumble backwards. I grabbed his arm and helped him catch his balance right before falling into a pile of rebar standing upright out of the concrete.

"Plan B?" I asked him.

"Do you have a Plan B because, if not, I'm gonna need a minute to think of something." Dante said looking around.

"Well, I thought the ceiling was higher but look, up near the hatch. The paint's peeling but it looks like it says twelve foot six inches. See, most of it is barely visible. That must be the clearance or ceiling height here."

"So?" Dante asked.

"So, maybe I can stand on your shoulders and reach the hatch, or…"

"Or, what?" he said clearly not liking the standing on his shoulder's idea.

"Or, we can try to pile some of this rubble together and climb up on it if we can get it high enough," I said. I knew this would take forever, but it might push him into considering me standing on his shoulders.

Now that I saw an exit, I wanted OUT OF HERE!

I also knew in Dante's mind this would mean I would get out and have to return to save him, not him save me. He wasn't going to jump on this idea. I wasn't up for the thought of either one of us having to stay in this tunnel alone waiting on the other one to come back.

"There's nothing substantial to stand on and most of what we've tripped over down here are old, rotted, pieces of wood. We'd need a truckload of rebar to tie together to climb up on. The concrete pieces are heavy and uneven. We could try that but let's walk a little farther along. Maybe there's another exit hatch with a ladder that isn't rust dust," he said. "Then we won't have to do a balancing act on debris and possibly fall and break something."

"Okay," I said, but mentally I would only give us about thirty minutes to find another hatch.

So, we plodded along the tunnel looking up, checking the ceilings for another opening, and the walls for another ladder. I thought the flashlight was dimming. I was stressed and fatigued so maybe I wasn't thinking or seeing clearly. The small flashlight had a strong beam when we started but it still only lit up an area about three square feet. We could easily miss finding another hatch or even finding the first one again.

While looking up I walked right into a giant, industrial, wooden spool.

"Whoa, look at this." I said.

"Spools of rope? In a tunnel? I wonder what they planned or used that for?" he muttered.

"At this point I don't care how this wasted the taxpayers' money. It's exactly what we need!" I said with renewed optimism.

"There's more than one," Dante said. "Maybe we can roll one back and stand on it."

That's what I was thinking but was glad he said it.

"Great idea. We can roll them back to the hatch. I hope they aren't as heavy as they look," I said.

We got one onto its side and rolled it back down the tunnel. Dante climbed up, but he was still not close enough to get any leverage to open the hatch.

"C'mon on," I said, "We need to get two more of those spools."

"Why?" Dante asked.

"Because, we need to put two as a base and get the third on top of them so you can climb up and reach that hatch," I said.

Before he listened to me and followed my suggestion aimlessly, he had to stand on the spool and see if he could reach the hatch. He couldn't.

"Let's go get two more spools," he said jumping down. "We'll try it your way."

My way being the only way.

Okay, I could have stood around dropping hints waiting for Dante to come up with this plan and he would have—sooner or later—but I wanted out of this tunnel. We were exhausted, and weak from lack of food. My clothes were ruined, and I was starting to think about a bathroom. We were right under civilization or as close to it as it gets in New Orleans, so why couldn't we get out of here? I felt punchy from no food, no water, no sleep, and the stress of being with someone who challenged every word I said.

It took us another hour to roll two more spools back to the first one. We set two side by side and then we had to heave one on top of those if we were ever going to climb high enough to get to the hatch. Dante and I had exact opposite ideas on how to do that so we wasted a lot of time trying it his way first.

His idea involved lifting this heavy spool on the top of the other two to create a pyramid. It didn't take him long to figure out I was the weak link in this plan.

Finally, after we both were exhausted and sat down to rest a minute.

"I have an idea," I said.

"Let's hear it, as long as it doesn't involve you lifting one end." He poked me in the ribs like he used to do when we were kids and he was teasing me.

"So, let's see if you, oh great Powerhouse, can lift one side while I shove a piece of wood or concrete under it. Then we both raise your side, turning it over so we use our strength as leverage. That way we are both lifting the weight from the same side. Once it's on its end, we let it fall on top of the bottom one." I said. I was using my hands rolling one over the other to demonstrate what I wanted to do.

"That might work," he said and flexed his arm as if showing off his bulging biceps.

The idea that we had a plan that could work and get us out of here gave us our second wind. Even though it was late, and we hadn't eaten or slept; we rallied.

We stood up and studied the three spools a minute. Dante picked the one he thought looked the lightest. The fact was, they all were exactly the same. Dante lifting one side for me to slide a scrap of two by four under wasn't the issue. That went pretty smooth. Now we had to turn this baby over itself to rest on top of the bottom spool.

"On the third breath," I said and counted after each deep inhale.

"What are you doing?" Dante asked me not moving to pick up his side with me.

"I see the body builders do this at the gym," I said. "They take three deep breaths and then on the third they do a heavy lift. One explained it helps oxygenate your muscles."

"All right, I'll give it a try," he said, and we both started taking deep breaths.

On the third, we lifted and pushed up the end on the ground, and somewhere in mid-roll when I felt the upward movement stop, we took another big, deep breath. With a big WHOOMP! the spool made the final turn and landed on top of the bottom one.

That sound gave us our second wind. Dante and I were scrambling on top of the bottom spools, then he climbed onto the top one. He reached the hatch and had to fight with it but finally pushed it open about an inch.

"It's so rusted, I'm not sure it will open anymore," he said.

"Wait," I said and rummaged through my purse. "I have a small can of silicone spray. It works like WD-40. Here," I said handing it up to him.

"Part of your lipstick survival kit?"

"No, I used it on equipment that gets stuck together at the office," I said. "It also cleans compartments where batteries have leaked or exploded—sometimes. I'll find you something you can try to pry it open with while that soaks the hinges."

I jumped down. I found a piece of rebar and brought it back to him. "Use this."

I stood on the ground holding my lipstick light on his workspace. Sticking the metal barb in the small opening, he worked at it until he pushed open the hatch completely.

I jumped around in a circle clapping my hands causing the light to bounce everywhere while I said, "Goody, goody, goody!"

"Can you control your enthusiasm? We aren't out yet. Shine your light up here so I can see what's above," he said.

The passage way was small, and I wasn't sure how Dante's large frame would squeeze through that hole.

"Let me see the light a minute. I can't tell what's above the opening," he said.

I handed it up and then kept my feet moving to keep anything near me from coming closer.

"We need to find some more wood or flat pieces of anything to stack on top of this spool. I need to raise my arms and get my head and shoulders clear of this opening to be able to pull myself through and then I can pull you up," he said. "I can see it widens and there's another ladder up above that looks like it leads to a manhole cover."

"I'll find some," scrambling down again to search in

the darkness. The flashlight was dimming. I had been wearing my purse across my body with the bag on my back so I could use my hands. I wondered it if was time to go to the cellphone flashlight. I didn't want to just yet. We didn't know what we would find when Dante climbed up that hatch. I hoped that manhole cover opened to somewhere, anywhere that got us out of here and not into another tunnel.

We found several pieces of cut lumber, much of it rotted but there were some useable parts that worked when we stacked them on top of each other. Stacking them the way Dante and I had seen bonfires built on the levees at Christmas made the pieces stronger and enough height for him to get his head and shoulders through.

"Please don't fall," I said as his head and arms disappeared into the hole. Then his legs wiggled before they shot up into the blackness and disappeared.

Frantically, I swept the light all around in the hole made by the hatch cover when suddenly it lit up Dante's big, smiling face.

When it was my turn for him to pull me up, I handed him the piece of rebar. "We might need it for the next hatch or manhole cover," I said. I don't want to come back down here."

He pulled me up into a space that was oval and about six feet high. We would hear the thump, thump of cars driving over the manhole cover above our heads.

"Great, we made it this far to lift that cover and get

our heads taken off by the front end of a car," he said.

"That's why I gave you the rebar. Push open the cover and hopefully, someone will notice so we can climb out."

He could reach the manhole cover with the rebar. When Dante moved the cover aside, a lot of light flooded into the hole we were standing in. We were under a street lamp! He jumped up grabbing the sides of the opening and pulled himself out. Then he pulled me up. When my head cleared the manhole, I looked right at the back entrance to one of the French Quarter coffee stands on Decatur Street.

Chapter Twenty

DANTE HAD TO hold me up because as soon as I stood up, my knees buckled and down to the pavement I went. I'm great in a crisis but once it's over, it seems all my resolve, and ability to stand leaks out through my feet. He picked me up and carried me over to a police car parked on the river side of the street. When he set me down on the hood of the police vehicle, the uniformed cop leaped out of the car.

Dante showed him his badge and introduced himself as Captain Deedler of the New Orleans Police Department Homicide Division.

By now, my legs were less rubbery, and I could stand on my own so I slid off the hood of the car. Digging my phone out of my purse and turning it on I noticed the time was 2:30 a.m. I caught a reflection of us in the police car windshield. We looked like the people living on the street in the French Quarter.

The uniform in the police car looked skeptical until Dante showed him his shield. Dante asked him to call the precinct and ask for Detective Hanky or Detective Taylor to come get us. He said either could confirm who we were. He briefed the officer on what had happened to us.

"Captain," the officer said as he opened the front passenger side door and back door for us to get in, "I'll take you."

"I'll ride in the back," he advised the uniform officer. "Let her have the front seat. Please take us to Police Headquarters on South Broad."

The uniform radioed Police Headquarters and Hanky and Taylor were waiting for us by the time we got there.

Detective Taylor looked me up and down noting the runs in my stockings, ripped skirt, filthy blouse, dirty face and the broken heel on one shoe. I also looked like I had been standing under a water hose. My hair and my clothes were sticking to my skin. Dante didn't look any better. We smelled like wet dogs.

"I understand people in New Orleans do all sorts of different activities for fun compared to what I did growing up in New York," Detective Taylor said while giving me the once over. "Did he take you to a tractor pull or did you go," then to Hanky he directed a question. "Hanky, what's it called...mudding?"

"No, he took me tunneling," I said with a straight face. "You should try it." I saw out of the corner of my eye Hanky turning away from us with a smile on her face.

Hanky, Taylor, and I followed Dante to his office so we could make formal statements and a complaint regarding the events from the day before. Neither of us saw who hit us with the Tasers, but we gave Taylor and Hanky the rundown on what we had been doing just before the kidnapping. Hanky immediately went off to get Ozzie's cellphone records and a printout of calls he made from his office phone. Dante Taylor to get Whit's computer from the Evidence Room to see if it was compromised.

I stood up. "I'll call a taxi to take me home," I said to Dante. "I need to call Suzanne and Jiff to let them know I'm alive."

"I'll take you home," Dante said. He stood up and walked over and wrapped his arms around me. "I'm glad I can still look forward to spending the rest of my life with you, even if we won't be together. I'm willing to wait for you, no matter how long it takes."

"Dante...I don't want..." I wanted to say I didn't want him to wait for me, but he cut me off.

"This isn't on you. I'm not going anywhere." Then he kissed me and I kissed him back knowing it was our last kiss.

I was glad the squad room outside Dante's office window was empty when Dante kissed me, but when our kiss ended, Taylor was standing in the doorway.

"Captain, the computer isn't in the Evidence Locker and it's not signed out." He held a sign-out form to Dante as we stood looking at each other after the kiss.

My eyes opened wider and Dante did an ever so slight shake of his head to warn me off saying anything about Ozzie or the missing computer.

"I'm not surprised. Just put that on my desk," Dante said but kept his eyes on me. Then, he kissed me again, a little less passionately, knowing Taylor was standing right there.

"Sure," Taylor said trying to find a way past the two of us still in an embrace. He finally set it on the credenza close to the door.

"Can you get a uniform to give me a ride home?" I asked Dante. "You probably want to go home too, unless you have things to do here."

"Yup, I need to finish up here." To Detective Taylor he said, "Taylor, assign a car to sit on her house tonight. Can you take her home and wait for one to show up?"

"Yes, I'll stay there tonight unless you want me back here," Taylor answered trying to decide where to look but mainly speaking to the floor.

"I'd appreciate it if you stay until a uniform arrives," Dante said. "Find a uniform you can trust with your sister."

"I'll wait for you at the elevator," Taylor said and left.

"I've seen how Taylor looks at you. If he ever tries anything and I find out about it, I'll shoot him," Dante said.

Dante walked me to the elevator where Taylor was waiting. He stood and watched us, well Taylor mainly, until we got in and the door closed.

"Wow!" Taylor said as soon as Dante was out of earshot, "I'll have to take a date and try this tunneling."

"Tunnel you," I said instead of 'screw you' and we both laughed.

Chapter Twenty-One

ON THE WAY to Taylor's car, I noticed he was a few steps behind me. I turned and saw him waiting with his cellphone to snap a photo of me looking like the wrath of God.

"You know, I have to say the word and Dante will shoot you," I said. "Now, delete that picture."

"No way. This is worth getting shot over," he said looking at the photo on his phone and showing teeth from east to west. "This is priceless."

"Your funeral," I said.

Once in his car I checked my messages and my phone lit up with calls and voicemails from Jiff and Suzanne. Voicemails and texts from Jiff said to call him and Suzanne. Messages from Suzanne asked me to let her know I was all right and to please call Jiff.

At 4:05 a.m. I called Jiff. He answered on the first ring. I told him I was fine and on my way home and would call him in a few minutes to let him know what happened. He asked if I wanted him to meet me at my house and I said it wasn't necessary. I told him there would be a police car in front of my house for the rest of the night. It was late; we were both tired, but he asked me to call once I was home. I agreed.

I texted Suzanne I was on my way home. She texted me back in less than a minute, Whew! Glad to hear it! You had us worried. Dogs are fine!

When Taylor drove up to my house, he jumped out and moved to open the passenger door for me. He followed me to the front door.

"Do you want me to check to make sure everything is all right?" he asked.

"I have a roommate who is home with two dogs who will bark their heads off if someone shows up," I said. As if on cue, the barking started inside. I could hear Justice and Meaux whining on the other side of the door. It felt good to be home, and I was eager for the wet nose welcome I was about to receive.

I thanked him for the ride and added, "If you don't delete that photo I'll tell Captain Deedler you tried to kiss me goodnight."

"Got it," he said holding his hands in surrender. He shook his head smiling at me as he turned to walk back to his vehicle. "I'll wait in the car until the detail gets here. There will be a car out here all night. If you need something…"

"Just that photo deleted," I said and barely had the energy to turn the key in the lock. What little energy I had left was melting out of my body. As my front door opened, I let the comfort of being home and my two dogs envelope me.

While I filled up my bathtub with hot water and bubble bath, I called Jiff back as I slid into the hot, therapeutic water, talking to him via blue tooth while I soaked. I remember telling him most of what happened and then I woke up in cold water about two hours later.

I dried off, and before I climbed into bed, I texted my assistant telling him I'd be in after lunch. I had a message from Dante asking me to come to his office before I went to work. He wanted to go over the information I had shared with him regarding what Mavis told me and what I remembered from Whit's computer. He asked me to bring the thumb drive.

The message I sent him back said I'd be there by 11:30 a.m. Then I played with Meaux and Justice, who had slept in the bed, one on either side of me, until I had to get up and get dressed to meet Dante.

Chapter Twenty-Two

WHEN I ARRIVED at the police station at 11:00 a.m., I was escorted to a conference room where Hanky, Taylor, three more detectives and Dante were already there waiting. They were talking to each other in what sounded like casual chit chat and not business.

"Let's get started," Dante said as he pulled out a chair for me to sit in and introduced everyone in the room. "As you know, Ms. Alexander and I were Tasered and thrown in one of the tunnels under the old Rivergate. We managed to find an exit and escape. I don't think the kidnappers wanted us dead because they had ample opportunity to kill us and dump us in the same place."

"So, they aren't pros," Taylor said.

"No, I don't think so. When we started to recover I found this copy of the note they left in my pocket."

"They left a note?" Hanky asked taking it from Dante. She read it before passing it around the table. It had COPY stamped on it. "Their printer could use toner," she said before handing it to Taylor. "What a bunch of rubes."

I smiled to myself.

"I'm having forensics run all the fingerprints from that note and some candy wrappers Brandy found to see if they are in the system. I'm not hopeful," he said.

The three detectives whom I had not met yet, Hanky and Taylor all shrugged or shook their heads as if thinking the same thing.

"Ms. Brandy Alexander is a consultant on this case since she knows the victim, Judge Whitmer," Dante said.

Hanky and Taylor looked at each other but made sure Dante was looking at his notes or me when they did it.

He continued, "And because we were both abducted right after we left headquarters yesterday. We had just left the Evidence Room after Ms. Alexander successfully logged into Judge Whitmer's computer."

"Ozzie couldn't hack it?" asked one of the three detectives I didn't know asked.

"I'll get to him in a minute," Dante said. He explained that he brought me here Wednesday and I found an application on Judge Whitmer's computer that tracked the whereabouts of his dog. "Before you start joking, the judge's dog was not at the crime scene when we arrived, but there were bloody paw prints around the body that didn't run away from it. Someone had to pick him and take him with them."

Hanky and Taylor were nodding in agreement.

"Since Brandy was at the crime scene, probably minutes after the murder and saw the judge earlier at Lancey's with his supporters, she has knowledge of the timeline from when Whitmer left Lancey's and was murdered.

She also looked at the computer program—a new tracking software not yet widely available—for keeping tabs on one's pet. When we left the station, and this is the last important piece, we were both hit by a Taser then left in one of the underground tunnels along the riverfront near the old Rivergate. She found something interesting while we were trying to find a way out. I'll let her tell you herself. Please hold questions to the end."

Shock didn't begin to describe what I felt with Dante including me in one of his briefings. Detective Taylor made a grand pretense of preparing to take notes. I could tell Hanky was as surprised as I was from the wide eyes she made at me right after she checked to see if Dante was watching.

"What is the time of death the coroner puts Judge Whitmer?" Dante asked of one of the three detectives.

Flipping through the file in front of him on the conference table he finally said, "Looks like the window is between 6:30 p.m. and 8:30 p.m."

"Brandy will give us information she has regarding who did what and when," Dante said. "We are hoping this will tighten the timeline on when the murder actually happened so we can get warrants to search cars and their GPS systems."

"I hope I can help you find who killed Judge Whitmer. Here's the timeline I put together from my arrival at Lancey's for his Judge Whitmer's party and I saw and spoke with him to when I found him dead and his ex-wife in his house. Times are approximate but close," I said as I passed around the copies I made earlier thinking Dante would ask me for a couple.

6:00 p.m. I arrived at Lancey's and the judge's party was in full swing.

6:30 p.m. Whit and Justine leave Lancey's w/golf buddies stopping Whit to talk, then leave right behind him.

6:50-7:00 p.m. Justine, his law clerk and soon to be wife number four—is seen by the neighbor dropping Whit off. (Does she go in?) No, according to Mr. Mouton/neighbor, leaves his home in his vehicle to pick up dinner and sees Justine drive off after dropping Whit. Then, Mr. Mouton sees another dark car drive up in his rear view mirror when he is a block away. He told me he knew it was not Justine returning as her vehicle was still in his line of vision ahead of him.

6:50 p.m. Marigny, Judge Martin's daughter, leaves her home to walk to Whit's house,

7:00 p.m. Mr. Mouton goes to pick up dinner, sees a dark car, black Mercedes drive off and one drive up. Mr. Mouton sees the same (?) black Mercedes there when he returned at 7:30 with dinner.

7:15 p.m. Uber receipt is for pick up on St. Charles and takes Marigny to Canal Street, near the cemeteries to a B&B. She needs a few minutes to walk/run to St. Charles and wait on Uber. Puts her at Whit's about 6:50 p.m., out by 7:00 p.m. or 7:05 p.m.

7:05-7:40 p.m. someone kills Whit (Person in black or dark sedan Mr. Mouton sees after Justine leaves and pulls up.)

7:30 p.m. Jiff and I leave Lancey's, separate and I head over to Whit's to return the jacket he left in the restaurant.

7:40-7:45 p.m. I arrive at Whit's house to find Claudette already there and Justice (dog) already gone.

7:40 p.m. Whit is dead when Brandy Alexander discovers the body

7:55 p.m. Bed and Breakfast on Canal Street has security footage that shows Marigny Martin arrive with Mavis Martin, her mother, waiting. Marigny hands her mother something that looks like a card, a note, or a photo.

8:04 p.m. Judge Martin arrives at Bed and Breakfast and takes Marigny home with him after a brief conversation with Mavis.

Everyone took a few minutes to read the timeline I passed around.

"You'll see it supports the coroner's TOD," Dante said. "Brandy, tell them about the judge's dog."

"I got a call the day after Judge Whitmer's murder from the New Orleans Animal Shelter to come get a dog registered to me. I do schnauzer rescue and this little dog's microchip was registered to me. They found him tied to the fence when an employee came into work. He was the schnauzer I adopted to Judge Whitmer three years ago," I explained. "Someone dumped him at the shelter tied to a fence in a puddle of water so any blood on him was all but gone."

"I don't think it was anyone's blood except the judge's anyway," Dante said. "Brandy, tell them about the tracking software."

By now, every time Dante tells me to give more information, Hanky and Taylor are looking at each other without the pretense of checking to see if Dante is looking at them.

"The computer showed the movements of Justice, that's the dog's name, that day from early in the morning until 8:15 p.m. when he was tied to the fence. There were two stops made after 7:30 p.m. with the dog in the car so there could be blood in someone's car. That car's GPS will show a route on the day of the murder from uptown to the bed and breakfast on Canal

Blvd where Mavis Martin, Judge Bas Martin's ex-wife is temporarily residing. The dog's tracker then shows he was driven to the West Bank Animal Shelter where it shows tracking him there at that location until I picked him up the next day. The trick will be to get the data off the GPS trackers in the suspects' cars. Those would be cars belonging to Judge Martin, Marigny Martin, Justine, the law clerk, August Randolph and Pierre LeBlanc or anyone else you think is a suspect. I believe it's one of these people."

One detective asked, "Are you sure it's not the ex-wife or the girlfriend?"

"We're sure it's not the girlfriend or ex-wife for the murder. We don't think Mavis Martin is the murderer since she is on a security tape, but she knows something," Taylor answered while Hanky nodded in agreement.

"We believe the judge had gambling debts regularly with members of his golfing partners. Judge Martin was one of the four. The two others are Pierre LeBlanc, a well-known surgeon, and August Randolph, the real estate developer," Dante said.

A collective groan went around the room at the mention of August Randolph's name.

"The GPS on someone's car will show that car went to the judge's house that evening. The dog's tracking program will show where it went and stopped until someone drove to the West Bank Animal Shelter. There's also the praline wrappers," I said. "There was one in the jacket pocket I was returning to the judge. We found the exact same wrappers in the tunnel. They were custom made to promote Judge Whitmer's campaign by the Randolph Companies LLC. They are a link to August Randolph and whoever dropped us in that tunnel."

"Wouldn't Randolph have a working knowledge of those tunnels since his casino sits on top of them?" Hanky asked.

"You know," Detective Taylor said, "someone kidnapped a member of law enforcement and a citizen, even though there was no ransom demand. I'm thinking the abduction was to warn you off the murder investigation."

"Wait. Maybe there was no demand because it wasn't about the money," Hanky said. "Maybe the two are unrelated."

"Missing money?" from one of the three.

"And the missing dog," I added.

Dante jumped in, "Yes, there was a wall safe in the judge's upstairs bedroom found open and empty when we arrived. At first, we thought it might be the ex-wife, but she seemed shocked at the death and there was no blood on her and no weapon."

"And no money," I said.

"Are we even sure there was money in that safe, and how much?" Taylor asked.

"Justine Wu, claimed she handled all his banking and bills," I said.

"Which one is Justine Wu?" one detective asked.

"Judge Whitmer's law clerk. The tall one with long dark hair," I answered.

"The ex-wives of both judges, the Martins' daughter and the law clerk are all tall with long dark hair," Taylor said. "Whitmer had a type."

"Jiff Heinkel and I spoke to Justine at the airport last Sunday and she claims she didn't know about the trust fund for the judge's two boys. I can't figure how she didn't know about it. If she really didn't know, and she was supposed to be marrying him, she might have felt he was holding out on her. She mentioned she always paid for everything. She also said the money was all cash and Whitmer told her it was about one hundred thousand for a business deal."

Dante added, "The gambling and money owed to different individuals makes them all suspects. The problem is one is a judge and the others are wealthy members of the community."

"If we haul them in, they'll all lawyer up. Judge Martin already has a lawyer," Hanky said. "For himself and his daughter."

"The other two will probably have someone on speed dial," I said. "You need a reason to impound their cars. Judge Martin, his ex-wife and their daughter are on that security video from the Canal Street Bed and Breakfast which shows their whereabouts during the timeframe of the murder."

Dante directed two of the three detectives to go do

an in-depth search on tickets, speeding, parking, anything on all the Martin, LeBlanc and Randolph family vehicles. "We might get lucky," he said.

"What about Ozzie, Captain? Do we want him to work on any of this?"

"No, he's meeting with Internal Affairs over the judge's missing computer from the Evidence Locker."

"If he's in cahoots with one of these guys we think is the murderer, then they would have known Judge Whitmer's passwords," Detective Taylor said.

"When I got back here Friday morning, after our tunnel trip," Dante said and looked at me with a slight hint of a smile, "I asked Detective Taylor to bring that computer in Evidence to me and it wasn't there."

"Captain Deedler indicated I should make a copy of the drive while we were looking at the judge's computer. Ozzie seemed to be paying attention to what we had found," I said. "We have proof of what was on the computer if anything is missing, or if it's been wiped."

Detective Taylor said, "Can I interrupt here for a minute? You're afraid these guys will lawyer up, right?"

"Right," Dante answered.

"Since they kidnapped a law enforcement officer we could call in the FBI," Taylor said. "The threat of the FBI wanting to speak with them if they don't speak to us might shake one of the loose."

"Let's see if they are willing to help us with this," Dante said. "I'll make the call and let you know when we will all meet back here."

Everyone got up and left with a specific task to follow up on. I walked over to Dante while he was picking up his papers and shoving them back in a folder.

"Here's your thumb drive," I said. "How did you know files or the computer would be missing?"

"Because it's not the first time its happened. Files are misplaced, misfiled, incorrectly labeled, lost, incomplete or lacking collected evidence or paperwork, and everything in between," Dante said. "Catching the bad guys is easy compared to this. If you have enough money and influence, you can pay off someone to help make sure your case is kicked out because the evidence can't be found."

Chapter Twenty-Three

FRIDAY FELT LIKE the longest day of my life. It was now almost 8:00 p.m. and I was home stretched out in one of my oversized chairs in the living room with my legs straight out, feet on the ottoman, arms outstretched on both sides with Meaux and Justice both sitting on top of me.

Jiff stood over me and offered to get me a glass of wine.

"As if being in the tunnels most of the night wasn't stressful enough, I didn't get much sleep before the meeting at the police station for the debriefing. Then I spent the afternoon trying to wrap up my office for the week after losing two full days at work. I am wiped out," I said.

"How about a glass of wine?"

"I'm so tired I don't think I could lift a glass of wine to my lips even if you got it for me," I said. "I'm sorry I'm not more fun, but I'll try to drink it if you pour it," I said smiling. "Am I smiling? I'm so tired I can't even tell."

"You should spend more time in those tunnels. It

has you very laid back," Jiff said over his shoulder as he left for the kitchen.

"I would if I thought it could help me figure out who killed Whit. What has me stressed is the fact I can't figure out who the murderer is. It's right in front of me, I know it."

"Maybe the tunnel experience has you a little off your game," Jiff said holding a chilled glass of Pinot Grigio. "Should I hold it to your lips to help you drink it like people do when they find someone in the dessert dying of thirst, or just dying?"

"No, give it here," I said taking the glass. "I'm missing something. If I find out what's missing, I might figure out who killed Whit then threw me in that tunnel. I realize this sounds bad, but right now I want who threw me in that tunnel more than I want Whit's murderer."

"One hand will wash the other. So, what are you missing?" Jiff asked.

"The money?" I said. "Two things said in that meeting today are key, but I'm still not seeing it yet. The first one is Hanky said what if the money and murder are not connected. The second thing Taylor said about Whit and that he definitely had a type, meaning all the women in the case look alike."

"Think outside the box, or in this case, outside the tunnel," Jiff said. When he saw the look I gave him, added, "Too soon?"

"Everyone I come up with that should be a suspect

doesn't need the money, or has a rock-solid alibi. Justine's family is in investment banking. Randolph is a big real estate investor with wads of cash, and Pierre LeBlanc is a well-known doctor and Bas Martin is a judge. None of these suspects need the money, or so it seems."

"Hanky could be right, and they aren't connected," he said.

That made me sit up and shoo the dogs off my lap.

"What if one of them didn't need the money or just wanted it, or felt they deserved it?" I said. "It's cash, so we'll never find it unless someone makes a huge deposit which seems unlikely due to the players involved. The timeline has always bothered me with the robbery and the murder at the same time. It seems either Claudette or I should have walked in on someone."

"Recap what you know," Jiff said squeezing in next to me on my oversized chair.

"Claudette, needed the money but I don't think she would empty the trust fund since it's for her sons' education. She's ditzy, but a good person deep inside. Mavis was the likely suspect for two reasons. One, she was the ex-girlfriend dumped before the ink on her divorce papers was dry. It ruined her marriage, and two, the nude photos pulled her daughter into the picture.

"Justine and August are investors. Since the market has been stable, neither of them seems to be jumping out of a window over a financial crash so they don't need the money," I said then stopped. "Remember, Justine was worried she wouldn't have a job now that Whit's gone? She said she had broken it off with him and went away for the weekend to avoid his calls. Why? She would have to see him on Monday if she assumed he was still alive, and I'm sure she did. She didn't even seem bothered by Whit's murder. She did seem annoyed over not knowing about the trust fund."

"Maybe, and you're right, she wasn't torn up over the news of his murder and she was very calm over the missing money," Jiff said.

"Pierre LeBlanc, is a well-known and successful plastic surgeon. Claudette said he joked that if Whit ever lost a bet to him, he would be happy to give Claudette "work" in trade, like a facelift or Botox," I said.

"Botox?" Jiff had his face all screwed up.

"It's for wrinkles," I said. "Don't worry about that right now."

"Or, what if Pierre was hit with a big malpractice suit? Then, he'd be interested in the money," Jiff said. "I'll get my investigator to check and see if he's involved in any lawsuits."

"Whoever took the money had to know it was there. Whoever killed him had to know he'd be alone at that particular time but didn't count on Claudette or me showing up." I mused over these two facts and what Hanky and Taylor had said in the meeting.

"Justine knew the money was there and how much.

Claudette hoped the tuition money was there, but she wasn't sure," Jiff said.

"Claudette hoped ten thousand in tuition money *might* be there. So she went looking because she was desperate to pay for her son's school so he wouldn't get kicked out. I don't make her the killer, but if she stole the money, she would have had it on her when we ran into each other and she didn't. Instead, she took me to the bedroom, showed me the safe which had already been opened and left empty. Justine not only knew it was there but how much. She saw it that morning."

"She doesn't strike me as the type to tolerate Whit's indiscretions or gambling vice. Would she kill Whit over it, or have him killed?" Jiff asked.

"I don't think Justine is the murderer but think how she acted over the money. Now…Justine could have taken the money when she left that house, most likely after Whit left for the courthouse. She leaves a few minutes later emptying the safe. She hit the jackpot with the murder that night. I'm sure the money was gone long before the murder took place. She felt Whit owed her. Remember, she complained she had to pick up the tab many times? Even thought he promised to pay her back, she said he never did. Her exact words were, 'I didn't need his money, he needed mine'". She said she realized she had no future with Whit and maybe the money was a self-awarded consolation prize? She paid all his bills, so she had to know where that money came from."

Jiff pondered that a few moments. "So, you think someone else killed Whit and sent those guys to throw you in the tunnel when they thought you could figure it out from the tracker app?"

"Yes, I do. I feel that these are two separate, unrelated incidents and that's what has had me confused. So that means the killer had a big interest in letting Whit's murder go unsolved, or let it get pinned on Clayton Haines. I have to go see Frank," I said jumping up and grabbing my purse.

"I'll drive you. You're exhausted, remember?" he said grabbing his jacket and running after me out the door.

Chapter Twenty-Four

MAVIS WAS SITTING on the front porch of Julia's Bed and Breakfast when we arrived. After our polite greeting we went looking for Frank, finding him heading out with a tray of two glasses of wine, one for Mavis and one for him.

"Frank, come right back and meet us in the Cone of Silence," I said.

"The what?" Frank looked confused.

"The closet," I said nodding it its direction.

I took Jiff by the hand and disappeared behind the door. While we waited for Frank and whatever persona he would arrive in, I showed him the escape hatch, Gloria's uniform, and the wig like hers with her cute housekeeper hat attached that were all stashed there for Frank's disguise.

Jiff was holding the wig when Frank joined us.

"Okay, Frank, did you tell anyone about this escape hatch other than me?"

"Well, Gloria knows. I told her in case she has to run interference if Julia sees me and thinks it's her leaving. I showed you," he said. "Now he knows," nodding at Jiff and rolling his eyes like it was some giant betrayal.

"Mavis? Did you show her before she started to kill a gallon of wine a day? I'm guessing that started after the judge was found murdered, right?" I asked staring at him.

"Well, I might have mentioned it to her and her daughter one day," he said.

"When? When did you mention it to them? How long ago?" I asked.

"It was a week or two ago. I wanted to entertain them. Marigny was visiting her mother, and they were both so sad and depressed, it was making me depressed and I'm normally a happy person," Frank said waving his arms around dramatically and knocking the wig out of Jiff's hand.

"When was this exactly?" I asked. "Before or after the judge was found murdered?"

"Oh, about two weeks before he was killed, on a Saturday afternoon. I remember because Marigny came to visit her mother and spent the night here," he said.

"That means everyone knows about this hatch except Julia, is that right?" I asked.

"More or less. But let that be our secret," he pleaded.

"I'll keep it a secret as long as I can," I said and suggested he slip out before Julia missed him.

I brought a copy of the FindMe path that Justice took on the night his owner was murdered. I showed it to Jiff. Justice's tracking program supported my theory.

"This isn't the happy ending I wanted for Bas and Marigny," he said.

"Or Mavis," I said.

I explained to Jiff what I thought happened. "Mavis had Marigny be the double for her at the B&B. Mavis slipped out the hatch and drove her car to meet her daughter somewhere within walking distance between the Martin home and Whit's. This way, Marigny could claim to have walked to Whit's, she drives her mother's car back to the B&B and slips in through the hatch.

"Mavis walked to Whit's house, demanded the photos, knew where he kept his gun in his desk and threatened him. Whit was drunk and probably belligerent, saying something insulting to Mavis regarding her age as compared to Justine's or worse, Marigny's. You know how Whit was when he found a chink in one's armor," I said.

"I can follow that logic, especially since he was drunk and Justine just dumped him," Jiff said.

"No doubt he provoked Mavis into shooting him when he wouldn't give up the photos and she confronted him over the call to Marigny to pose for him. I think Randolph was key into letting Mavis know when Whit would be alone. He either followed Justine and saw her leave without going in, or Justine gave him a heads up she was leaving Whit. I'm betting he was waiting out front for Mavis to give her a ride back to the B&B. It was his car Mr. Mouton saw.

"I bet he told her to shoot Whit fifteen times to look like the gang hit. The wild card came into play when Mavis took Justice with her when she walked out so he wouldn't bark or run out with the blood all over him." I said.

"Randolph knew exactly when Whitmer would be alone," Jiff said.

"Yes, and he also drives a black Mercedes," I said. "August Randolph makes sense because of the real estate connection."

Jiff said. "I always felt he made some unsavory investment deals over the years. He was always on the front end of property sales, bankruptcies and tax sales."

"I think Mavis got in Randolph's car with Justice and then they had to figure out what to do with him. This accounts for the two stops on this path the tracker shows," I said. "It's around the corner from Whit's house. Maybe she walked out with the dog and the car followed her to a point away from Whit's house so as not to be detected. Mavis left the dog with him with instructions to take Justice to a shelter. Then she took the Uber back to the B&B making an appearance like she was Marigny. Instead, I think Randolph followed Mavis back to the guest house to make sure she gets here like she is supposed to. His GPS would show the route the tracker shows with Justice going from Whit's house uptown to here in Mid City, then back across town and over the river to the West Bank Shelter. Mavis probably called Bas when she was almost to the guest house saying Marigny came to see her after arguing with Whit."

"That gave her the alibi, and they were dressed alike, all in black, no one looked at Mavis' clothes, only her daughter. Marigny leaves with Bas, Mavis gets rid of the clothes if they have blood on them," Jiff said. "Randolph takes the dog and the gun to dispose of."

"I'm guessing Randolph would have contacts in construction to find guys to abduct Dante and me," I said.

"Yes, and I bet he knows all about those tunnels under the casino since he was the one who financed its construction. It bears following up on, which you should let the police do," Jiff said and pulled me in close for a hug.

"I will," I said. "It's time to call Dante."

"I could have lost you in those tunnels and never seen you again, or even known what happened to you," he said, hugging me tighter.

Chapter Twenty-Five

JIFF AND I met Dante at his office. It was past ten o'clock, but he was still there. I gave him my theory, showed him the printout of the FindMe path Justice took that night. I told him my theory that the money and the murder weren't connected.

"Hanky's been saying that too," he said. "It just didn't fit the timeline. This printout is the missing piece I needed to get warrants. The detectives found two things. One was on the security video from Julia's bed and breakfast. Right after Mavis Martin checked in she had a visitor. It was August Randolph. Then we found a connection between Judge Martin, August Randolph and Ozzie. This is the icing on the cake."

Was this an acknowledgment that I helped? Jiff and I looked at each other.

"August Randolph had been doing Bas and Mavis favors over the years, like getting Mavis' DUI evidence to vanish. There were several. Randolph had Ozzie, his cousin, working in Evidence and on the favor payroll. Randolph made a call to Ozzie and evidence promptly disappeared or was compromised," Dante explained.

"So, August does these sorts of favors for the Martins for favorable outcomes with any hearings pertaining to his permits or construction variances, right?" Jiff said.

"Yes, and Bas called in favors or twisted the arms of friends in the right places when necessary to help get what Randolph wanted. Ozzie spilled it all when threatened with jail time," Dante said. "When Ozzie thought we might figure out the computer tracking program he panicked. He called Randolph. Ozzie knew we saw it and told Randolph he hadn't had time to get rid of the computer."

"August sent two thugs to scare us off Judge Whitmer's murder. It gave Ozzie time to get rid of the computer, and without the computer he knew the police would have to drop the case or it would be an unsolved "Clayton Haines" murder. He didn't figure on you making a copy."

"They could have killed you both if you never found your way out of those tunnels," Jiff said. "They are collapsing in several places."

"Well, I'm glad I didn't know that while I was down there," I said. "Dante, the porn is still on that thumb drive."

"I'd like to leave it out. Since the computer has vanished, we can say the porn doesn't exist," Dante said. "That will save face for Judge Martin and his daughter. While we don't see how Judge Martin was involved with the murder, Mavis Martin will be charged and it will look like a crime of passion. Randolph will be an accomplice and charged with kidnapping a police officer and a citizen.

"We are waiting to see what the D.A. wants to do about Marigny, since she's a minor and was coerced by her mother. We think Mavis handed Marigny the Uber receipt on that tape. We thought it was a photo."

Dante stood up and thanked us. He thanked me for harping on the dog and finding the tracking software.

"You know, using you as a consultant has its merits," he said. "I'll be calling you again, if you are willing."

"I'm willing to help wherever I can. You know, most of the time I'm already at the crime scene before you show up," I said smiling. "You won't even have to call me since I'm usually there already."

AFTER WE WERE in the car heading home, I noticed Jiff seemed a little tense.

"What's up?" I asked.

"I don't like him asking you to be a consultant. That's his way of keeping you in his life," he said. "You'll do what you want anyway, but I don't like it, I just don't like it."

Imagine how much he wouldn't like it if he knew Dante had run background checks on him and his family looking for an excuse to arrest them and throw them in jail!

"I like being your consultant more," I said taking one of his hands that were clenched onto the steering wheel to hold. "I wouldn't worry about it."

The End

These are the BEST Pralines I have ever had.

My Mother's PRALINE RECIPE

1 Candy thermometer

1 cup brown sugar

1 ½ cup white sugar

½ cup cream (my mother used canned cream but you can use fresh Heavy Cream)

3 Tablespoons butter

1 ½ cups peeled pecans (some pieces, some whole-your preference)

Dash vanilla

Mix and cook sugar and cream until hard boil stage.

Stir in butter and pecans and cook again to hard boil stage.

Do not beat. Pour by spoonful on waxed paper. Let cool.

I LOVE TO HEAR FROM FANS SO DROP ME AN EMAIL, OR STAY IN TOUCH ANY OF THESE WAYS:

Join my newsletter/website – I promise I only send out emails once or twice a month AND you will get hear about other deals from my Author friends:

My website:

www.colleenmooney.com

Email:

colleen@colleenmooney.com

Facebook:

facebook.com/colleen.mooney.716

BookBub:

bookbub.com/profile/colleen-mooney

Twitter:

twitter.com/mooney_colleen

Instagram:

instagram.com/colleen.mooney

Goodreads:

goodreads.com/author/show/8548635.Colleen_Mooney

Amazon:

amazon.com/Colleen-Mooney/e/B00N9I5DMK

If you like my books, please consider giving me a five star review on Amazon. If you don't like them, let me know why!

Thanks,
Colleen

Many of you know I do breed rescue for schnauzers, like Brandy! Here is My Schnauzer Rescue Facebook page. Check us out and post photos of your BFF-he or she does not have to be a Schnauzer!
facebook.com/NOLASchnauzerRescue

Our Schnauzer Rescue of Louisiana aka NOLA Schnauzer website:
www.nolaschnauzer.com

RESCUE ONE TIL THERE'S NONE!

Made in the USA
Middletown, DE
14 March 2019